"Please..." The sound of her voice whispered in the air between them.

Please, what? Please turn around and go away? Please pretend you didn't find me? Please don't take my only chance at freedom away from me?

The man flipped a switch and the sudden light made Amanda squeeze her eyes closed.

"Mrs. Stowe, I don't appreciate having to chase you up the stairs and through the halls before I've even had my morning coffee. Why don't you just settle down and come to grips with the fact that your running days are over?"

The weary, steel tone in his voice gave credence to his words. Now that she could see him in the light, her gaze flew to his face. The dark eyes glaring back at her confirmed her fears that there would be no room for negotiations, but still she had to try.

"Please, you're making a mistake. I didn't kill my husband."

grinned. "I told you to use the booze and knock her out."

Books by Diane Burke

Love Inspired Suspense

Midnight Caller
Double Identity
Bounty Hunter Guardian

DIANE BURKE

is the mother of two grown sons and the grandmother of three wonderful, growing-like-weeds grandsons. She has two daughters-in-law who have blessed her by their addition to her family. She lives in Florida, nestled somewhere between the Daytona Beach speedway and the St. Augustine fort, with Cocoa, her golden Lab, and Thea, her border collie. Thea and Cocoa don't know they are dogs, because no one has ever told them. Shhhh.

When she was growing up, her siblings always believed she could "exaggerate" her way through any story and often waited with bated breath to see how events turned out, even though they had been present at most of them. Now she brings those stories to life on the written page.

Her writing has earned her numerous awards, including a Daphne du Maurier Award of Excellence.

She would love to hear from her readers. You can contact her at diane@dianeburkeauthor.com.

BOUNTY HUNTER GUARDIAN

DIANE BURKE

Love Inspired

Recycling programs
for this product may
not exist in your area.

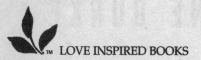

™ LOVE INSPIRED BOOKS

ISBN-13: 978-0-373-44467-0

BOUNTY HUNTER GUARDIAN

The Lord is my strength and shield.
I trust him with all my heart.
—*Psalms* 28:7

To Connie Mann and Kit Wilkinson,
great authors and good friends.
You've been with me each step of the way
no matter what I need or when I need it.
Thanks, gals!

ONE

Amanda Stowe sprinted past the evergreen garlands tucked around the doorways of the bed-and-breakfast. Who would have believed that a building that stretched the length of two city blocks could be found out here smack-dab in the middle of nowhere? The grand and imposing hotel had been at least an hour's drive north of Fairbanks. But the isolation was probably its biggest draw—Alaskan wilderness the safe way.

Amanda didn't feel very safe at the moment.

She barely registered the fresh scent of pine that tickled her nose as she raced on, ducking down one hall, running as fast as she could down another. Turning the last corner, her eyes widened as she spied the gaily decorated Christmas tree standing like a sentinel at the top of the stairs and prayed she'd be able to stop before she slid into it like a baseball player stealing home plate.

Slow down. Get control of yourself.

She heeded the stern voice in her head and stopped running before she drew unwanted attention to herself or, worse, crashed into the tree looming now only a couple dozen yards ahead.

She stole a moment to check behind her. She was still safe. The hall was empty.

Panting heavily, she tried to catch her breath and continued to move forward. This time instead of an all-out run, she chose what others might call "a purposeful stride." If anyone saw her hurry by, they'd probably think she was late for breakfast or, maybe, for one of the many Alaskan tours the facility offered.

She clenched her sweaty palms and forced herself to try and breathe normally. She could do this. She just had to stay composed and think things through calmly and logically.

Amanda groaned aloud when she realized she was subconsciously humming under her breath to the piped-in Christmas music in spite of her high level of anxiety.

Christmas was the last thing that should be on her mind. She was running for her life.

She threw another nervous glance over her shoulder. She paused in the hallway just long enough to turn a doorknob in search of the impossible—an unlocked door.

She couldn't believe her luck when the knob twisted beneath her grasp and the door eased open. She thanked the good Lord that this bed-and-breakfast was tucked away in a remote area of Alaska. She'd never have found sanctuary without a magnetic key card back in "civilization."

She ducked into the dimly lit room and crouched in a ball at the foot of the bed. Pulling her coat over her head, she hoped if the man following her did happen to glance inside that he'd mistake her for nothing more than a discarded blanket in the darkness.

Agonizing seconds beat past as she stared with one eye out of a buttonhole, never taking her attention from the door.

Nothing.

No one.

A wave of hope washed over her, and a smile tugged at

the corner of her mouth. She counted silently to herself. One one hundred. Two one hundred. Three one hundred.

Still nothing.

She'd given him the slip. She was sure of it.

Or not.

Before she dared to celebrate, she heard footsteps pause outside the room.

Seconds felt like hours as she held her breath. She wished she could just close her eyes and disappear. She didn't dare move or even blink.

Go away. Please, Lord, don't let him find me.

The doorknob turned.

Amanda's shoulders sagged with defeat. This couldn't be happening. She couldn't be this close and have to watch it all slip right through her fingers.

Backlit from the light in the hall, the man's shadow preceded him into the room, stretching so far across the floor in front of her that she swore he must be a giant. Her heart skipped a beat—maybe two.

When she dared to glance his way, she was certain her heart ceased beating all together. He was huge. His body filled the doorway so completely she figured he had to be at least six foot four or more. His shoulders, enclosed in a heavy, thick coat actually brushed the sides of the door frame. His cowboy hat rode low over his face masking his features in the room's darkness.

"Please…" The sound of her voice whispered in the air between them. *Please, what? Please turn around and go away? Please pretend you didn't find me? Please don't take my only chance at freedom away from me?*

The man flipped a switch, and the sudden light made Amanda squeeze her eyes closed.

"Mrs. Stowe, I don't appreciate having to chase you up the stairs and through the halls before I've even had my morning coffee. Why don't you just settle down and come to grips with the fact that your running days are over."

The weary, steel tone in his voice gave credence to his words. Now that she could see him in the light, her gaze flew to his face. The dark eyes glaring back at her confirmed her fears that there would be no room for negotiations, but still she had to try.

"Please, you're making a mistake. I didn't kill my husband."

Chance Walker studied the petite woman. Slowly she rose from her ridiculous crouched position by the bed and now stood in front of him. She was five-two, maybe five-three, and probably weighed one hundred pounds soaking wet. Had she really believed he wouldn't see her curled up in a ball? Was that jacket supposed to be an invisible cloak or something? He shook his head. He was tired—dog tired. Hide-and-seek with criminals didn't do it for him anymore.

Dressed in layers of clothing—a turtleneck beneath a heavy leather jacket, designer jeans and boots—with thick, chestnut hair gathered in a ponytail and brown eyes pleading with him beneath long, curled lashes, she looked like a model on a shoot instead of the bail jumper that she was.

"Put your arms behind your back." He released the handcuffs from his belt.

Amanda held her palms out and took a step back. "Please, you don't understand. You can't take me back. Not yet. I know who killed Edward. I just need a day or two to prove it."

"That so?" He adjusted his cowboy hat, let out a weary-sounding sigh and took a step toward her. "Tell it to the judge."

"Give me a day. Only one day," she pleaded, backing

up a little more. "You can come with me. You can keep an eye on me the entire time. After we get the evidence I need, I'll go with you—without protest or problems. I promise."

"Lady, you're going with me *now*. And I can guarantee you that no matter how much you protest there won't be any problems. Now turn around and put your hands behind your back."

Amanda paled and froze in place.

She looked at him like a deer in the headlights of an oncoming car, and a wave of pity washed over him. Instead of endearing him to the woman, though, the empathetic feelings angered him. Feelings had no place in this business—especially ones that painted a criminal as anything other than a lying, manipulative lowlife. It was past time that he got out of this business. He was burned out. He couldn't trust his judgment anymore.

He lifted his hat, raked a hand through his hair and lowered it back on his head. This was the last time. He was leaving the bounty hunter business for good and opening his own security firm. He'd be happier telling individuals and corporations how to keep themselves safe and prevent crimes rather than chasing the bad guys—or gals—after the fact.

He'd almost turned this job down. But the money was too good to pass up—four times his normal finder's fee. Combined with what he'd already saved, he'd have enough money to leave this life behind and get his security business off the ground.

"Please…" Her word was a mere whisper, almost as if she knew it carried no weight but couldn't resist trying anyway.

Who was she kidding? The daughter-in-law of a Supreme Court judge nominee, Amanda Stowe undoubtedly knew she was front page news. There was a national warrant out for her arrest. He couldn't afford to give her the day or two she requested. With the dollar signs on her head, every professional law-enforcement officer, every detective—amateur and otherwise—and even news hounds would be looking for her. If any of them got a whiff of her location, they would be descending on them in a heartbeat. He had to get her out of Alaska and back to the Virginia courts, and he had to do it fast.

"Look, lady, you can do this under your own power or not. It's your choice." He lowered his voice and made it as stern as possible. "Turn around. Now."

The fight went out of her. Her shoulders slumped. Her head lowered and she turned around slowly. She winced when he pulled her hands behind her back and clamped the cuffs in place but didn't try to resist.

"Let's go." He held on to her arm and steered her toward the door.

The bail bondsman had arranged their transportation. Chance knew that leasing a private plane was a lot cheaper than forfeiting the quarter of a million dollars the bondsman stood to lose if she didn't show up in court.

Chance mentally calculated the time it would take them to grab a quick bite to eat in the hotel dining room versus leaving right away and then figured it was worth the risk. If they grabbed a quick bite to eat now, they wouldn't have to stop later. He'd have her returned to custody and he'd be on his way home by nightfall.

It didn't matter if the tiny woman didn't look like she could hurt a fly let alone murder her husband. It didn't matter if her eyes reached in and tugged at his heartstrings, confusing him, making him want to hear her story and maybe even help.

He clenched his teeth and almost let out a low growl.

Knock it off. What's got into you?

Amanda Stowe had jumped bail. Period. He had never let a bail jumper get away—and he wasn't about to start now.

Amanda twisted her wrists in a futile attempt to loosen the handcuffs, but the effort only resulted in chafing and more discomfort. Now she knew how a wolf felt with its leg caught in a steel trap. The only thing on her mind was escape. But how?

Her eyes fixed on her captor. His longish black hair brushed against the collar of his thick, heavy coat. Darkened stubble covered the lower half of his face. Coal-black eyes stared back at her. If the situation wasn't so tragic, she'd find it humorous. Here was the hero she'd read about in many of her romance books—tall, dark and dangerous.

Only now she wasn't reading a book, and there was nothing funny about the situation.

His large hand wrapped itself in a firm grip around her arm. He stood so close that the warmth of his breath fanned her face. Amanda knew her life couldn't be more threatened if she'd come face-to-face with a grizzly bear.

"We'll stop by your room and get your things before we go downstairs." He gently pushed her toward the door.

"I…I don't have a room here. I only came here to meet someone. My belongings are at a hotel in Fairbanks. We need to go there to pick them up."

The man tipped his hat back with his free hand and stared at her with a look of astonishment on his face. A chuckle escaped his lips.

"You think I'm stupid, don't you? You're stalling. Hoping when we reach a more populated area that somehow you'll be able to give me the slip."

His sudden forward momentum forced her to back up against the door frame. He came threateningly close.

"Don't mess with me, Mrs. Stowe. I'm not in the mood."

"Amanda." She winced at how the word croaked out of her throat in a whimper instead of the firm declaration of power she'd hoped to portray. Her legs trembled with fear and she couldn't seem to catch her breath, but no way was she going to let him know how terrified she was. She straightened as tall as her five-two frame would allow and stared back at him.

"My name is Amanda." She'd read somewhere once that if you were faced with a violent enemy you should personalize yourself. You should get them to see you as an individual instead of a means to an end.

His eyebrow arched. Walker stared at her like she was an unknown species that intrigued him and annoyed him simultaneously.

"Okay. I'll call you anything you want me to call you… Amanda. Just move. Now."

Gently but firmly he propelled her into the hallway. Without any input from her, in less than a minute he had steered them directly to her room, opened the door and ushered her inside.

Her stomach twisted in knots. No wonder he'd laughed when she tried to get him to take her to Fairbanks. He'd done his homework. He knew she'd been lying about not being a guest at the lodge. He arrived at her room as if he'd been there before. He probably had. After they entered, he made her stand in the far corner, placing himself between her and freedom.

Good. He must think she'd try to escape. She had no intention of trying to make a run for it. But just the fact that he thought she was clever enough to try boosted her self-confidence. He might be willing to negotiate her freedom if he came to believe she'd escape anyway. Maybe if she attempted a tougher persona he'd see her as a viable adversary who just might get away. If he believed he was going to lose her anyway and she could get him to listen to her—or at least to her money—he might be willing to accept a sizable payoff to let her go.

"Who are you? What's your name?" she asked as she watched him grab her suitcase out of the closet and toss it on the bed.

He shot a glance her way. "Chance Walker. I'm a bounty hunter."

Bounty hunter? Not a federal marshal or local law-enforcement officer? Her hopes rose. Maybe money would work after all. If only she could get her hands on some. Most of her assets were frozen. Did bounty hunters accept IOUs?

She watched as the man grabbed her clothes out of the closet and shoved them into her suitcase.

How could she exude a sense of power and control when she cowered in the corner with her hands fastened behind her back? Got it! She'd imitate her mother-in-law. The woman always intimidated her.

"Didn't your mama teach you how to fold your clothes?" She put as much derision into her tone as she could muster, even raised her chin a bit so she could look down her nose at him.

He arched an eyebrow and froze. Instead of intimidating him, her words seemed to anger him more.

"Well *excuse* me. I forgot. You think you're some high-class lady and your money entitles you to demand people do your bidding. Well, I'm not one of your servants." His tone of voice lowered to a growl. "And *you're* no lady. You're nothing more than a criminal who tried to escape justice."

They stared at each other in silence. The tension in the room was almost palpable.

His eyes narrowed. "So I'll pack your clothes any way I see fit. You have no room to ask me for favors or anything else for that matter. Understand?"

She clamped her jaw shut to still her chattering teeth but didn't turn away from his cold, hard glare. For once, she was glad her hands were behind her back and he couldn't see her trembling.

When he seemed satisfied she wasn't going to argue with him any further, he turned and picked up a Bible, which had fallen to the floor, and started to put it inside the nightstand.

"That's mine," she informed him.

He glanced from her to the book in his hand and back again. "Yours?"

"Yes."

"I thought it was just one of those books you see in all hotel rooms."

"It's not. It's mine, and I'd appreciate it if you'd pack it carefully." She swallowed the tough guy persona act. It wasn't working anyhow. "Please."

He stared at her for a moment. "Do you read this thing?" He held it up in the air.

"Every day."

"Didn't learn much from it, did you?"

Amanda huffed out an annoyed breath but refrained from allowing him to bait her.

He turned back to the job at hand.

After a minute or two, as she watched, a smile threatened to pull at the corners of her mouth. She couldn't help but note that despite his angry words and threats this big, fierce, nonrelenting male packed the remainder of her belongings with much more care.

Chance tucked her suitcase awkwardly under his right arm and looped the strap of his own duffel bag that had been sitting in the hall on the floor outside her room over his head. He clasped Amanda close to him with his left hand. "Let's get a move on."

Step by step they made their way down the stairs.

The sound of clinking glasses and people's voices grew closer as they neared the bottom of the stairwell. They stepped around the massive, beautifully decorated Christmas tree in the foyer and found themselves in the entranceway to the dining room.

Several dozen tables were scattered throughout the room. They were covered with white, hand-embroidered tablecloths, and the metallic shimmer in the threads made each table shimmer and appear like delicate snowflakes tumbling to the floor. The tops of the tables were decorated with evergreen sprays filled with red candles and dancing snowmen. The far wall of the restaurant was solid glass with a breathtaking view of the distant mountains. The pane glass was etched with snow. A large, glowing fireplace claimed a focal point in the room, and Amanda thought the whole thing was one of the loveliest sights she'd seen in a very long time.

Moving to the nearest empty table, the bounty hunter deposited her suitcase and his bag on the floor, sat down and gestured to the chair opposite him.

Amanda's cheeks flamed with embarrassment as the patrons noted her handcuffs. Low murmurs of excited and speculative whispering filled the room. If looks could kill, she'd have just shot Chance Walker a lethal dose. She stood beside the empty chair and glared at him.

"How am I supposed to eat with my hands cuffed behind my back? Or am I just expected to sit and watch you?"

He tipped his chair back on two legs and grinned up at her. "Say please."

He stood up, came around the table and released the cuffs.

Instantly, she rubbed her right wrist with her left hand. Those bracelets hurt!

Before she knew what was happening, he had cuffed her left wrist to one of the spindles of her ladder-back chair and had returned to his seat.

"This is ridiculous," she hissed, leaning across the table and hoping the entire room wouldn't eavesdrop on their conversation. "You're treating me like a common criminal."

"That's what you are."

"I'm not." Hot tears burned her eyes. Angry that she allowed him to glimpse this sign of weakness, she forced her tone of voice to remain stoic and calm. "You'd realize you're making a huge mistake if you'd just give me the opportunity to explain."

His eyes shuttered, and he ducked his face behind a menu. "I'd suggest you order a hearty breakfast. We're not stopping for lunch or anything else. We're going straight from here to jail. Do not pass go. Do not collect $200. Isn't that how the game is played?" he asked. "Besides, I doubt you'll have any appetite once I return you to custody."

Her stomach lurched. She couldn't let him take her back. She had to meet with the woman who held the evidence she needed to clear her name. She needed a plan. But what?

"Well? Are you going to order, or are you just going to sit there and starve?" His dark eyes caught hers over the top of the menu, and she felt inexplicably drawn to the strength and control she saw in them.

"Makes no mind to me whether you eat or not," he said

with a shrug. "But I'm hungry. After chasing you through the hallways, I worked up an appetite. I'll order for you. If you don't eat, that's just more for me."

She fought the overwhelming urge to kick him in the shin as hard as she could.

The waitress timidly approached their table, rarely taking her eyes off Amanda's handcuffs as she asked for their order.

Chance seemed oblivious to Amanda's discomfort or of the murmurs and glances from the other patrons. And, obviously, he didn't give a hoot about how humiliating this was for her.

The aroma of fresh coffee, homemade bread and cinnamon buns wafted to the table, and her stomach growled loudly in anticipation. She *was* hungry. She hadn't eaten dinner last night or lunch before that, but she hated giving him the satisfaction of being right.

Chance ignored her silence and ordered enough to feed a small army—eggs, meat, pancakes, potatoes, toast, fresh baked bread, an order of cinnamon rolls and coffee. He wasn't kidding. He didn't intend any detours or stops once they left the inn. This was going to be a direct, one-way ticket to jail the second this breakfast was over.

After the food was delivered, Amanda bowed her head and prayed a blessing.

"What are you doing?" Chance stopped his fork halfway to his mouth. An astonished expression crossed his features. He glanced around as though she had purposely done something to embarrass him.

"I'm saying a prayer of thanksgiving for my food." This was the first time she'd seen any sign of discomfort in him, and it intrigued her.

"Well, stop it." He glanced side to side, ducked his head and continued to eat his breakfast.

"Don't you pray, Mr. Walker?"

"Prayer is for fools who need a crutch in life. I'm no fool."

For the first time since she'd laid eyes on him, a wave of sympathy washed over her. Instead of criticizing him or contradicting him, she lowered her eyes and continued her prayer.

"If you're going to be doing that, do it silently," he ordered.

She blinked in amazement. Dragging her into the restaurant in chains—okay, he didn't drag her and it wasn't chains but handcuffs, but still—none of that seemed to bother or embarrass him. But show devotion to the Lord and boy, did he squirm. Interesting.

Respecting his discomfort, Amanda finished her blessing in silence. Her stomach growled again, and she didn't need any further encouragement to dig into the spread before her. After all, she had to keep her body fit, her mind alert if she stood any chance of escape—even though logic told her that escape was impossible.

All things are possible with God.

She smiled. It was true. God could do anything. She offered up another silent prayer, this time for help, even as she shoved a forkful of eggs into her mouth and tried not to show how delectable everything tasted.

A man moved deeper into the shadows of the hallway. He hid behind the Christmas tree at the base of the stairs, removed the prepaid cell phone from his pocket and dialed. It was answered on the third ring.

"Talk to me."

He ducked his head and cupped his hand over the mouthpiece so his voice wouldn't carry to the diners. He peered through the branches, moving his head until he had an unrestricted view. "They're here. That Walker guy is sitting less than fifty feet from me, and he has the woman with him."

"Take care of it."

Before he could reply, the person on the other end of the line hung up.

TWO

Amanda studied Chance over the rim of her cup before taking a sip of her coffee. His cowboy hat showed considerable wear, rode low on his forehead, hiding all of his black hair except the longish strands that brushed his collar. His nose, broad and slightly crooked, looked like it had been the recipient of more than a fist or two. The dark stubble covering the lower half of his face gave him a rakish appearance. And those eyes—they stared at her with an intensity that took her breath away.

She felt her face flush with warmth and lowered her head with guilt. She'd been a widow for seven months. It didn't matter that she'd only been married twelve weeks before Edward had been killed. She shouldn't be noticing anything about any man—let alone one who was trying to put her in jail.

Walker was like a heat-seeking missile focused on his target. No matter which way the target veered or tried to maneuver out of his path, Walker would find and destroy it. A sinking feeling in her stomach reminded her that *she* was his target. Her attempt to intimidate him earlier had failed miserably. She'd have to try something else. But what?

"It's time to go." Chance wiped his mouth with a napkin, tossed it on the table and rose.

"I'm not finished."

"You're finished. Let's go."

Amanda's heart beat in a wild rhythm. He was taking her in. When the mental picture of an orange jumpsuit and prison bars popped into her mind, she almost hyperventilated. Now she'd never get her hands on the evidence she needed to clear her name.

She folded her hands on her lap. "You said we wouldn't be stopping to eat anymore today." She raised her eyes to his. "Can't I finish my breakfast?"

He glanced at her half empty plate and muttered something under his breath. Dropping down onto his chair, he folded his arms across his chest and didn't say a word. He didn't have to. His face said it all. Impatience. Anger. Frustration. Tinged with what? Pity? Empathy? Human kindness?

Amanda offered him a weak smile, lowered her gaze to her plate and picked up her fork. Nervousness constricted her throat muscles, and she was certain she wouldn't be able to swallow. At this point, choking to death seemed a welcome alternative to life in prison. Stealing a glance at the bounty hunter, she groaned inwardly. Nah, choking wouldn't work. This guy would know the Heimlich.

"How long have you been a bounty hunter?" she asked and then forced a forkful of food into her mouth.

"Too long."

She took her time chewing then tried to swallow, surprised when it went down. "Have you ever turned in an innocent person before?" She braced herself for an angry outburst, but it didn't come.

"Innocent people don't run." He tilted his chair on its back legs, rocking it slightly.

"I am innocent." She dropped her fork on her plate. "And I didn't run."

He arched an eyebrow and allowed his chair to right itself. "Your bail was set at a quarter of a million dollars. There has to be some pretty hard evidence against you to warrant numbers that high."

Amanda lowered her eyes and remained silent.

"If I remember the news reports correctly, your husband was found shot to death in your own bed. The police responded to a 911 call and found you covered in his blood. Your fingerprints were on the gun—a gun registered to you, I might add. There were no signs of forced entry into the house. And, oh yes, you didn't have an alibi. How am I doing? Got the facts straight?"

Amanda blanched but continued to remain silent.

Chance adjusted his hat, leaned forward with both elbows on the table and in a conspiratorial whisper said, "But there's more, isn't there, Mrs. Stowe? For your bail to be that high the district attorney has to feel he has a slam-dunk case against you. What's the missing piece of the puzzle? Motivation, maybe? Can they prove why you killed Edward?"

Pain seeped through every pore of her body as images of that night flashed through her mind and she had to fight to keep from sobbing. She raised her eyes to his. "You don't understand. I can explain everything."

"Of course you can. That's why you ran."

"I didn't run."

He sat back and spread his arms wide as if to encompass the room. "Yet, here you are."

"I had to meet someone. I had a limited amount of time to do it. I didn't have time to get the court's permission or I would have."

Chance glared at her, his tone of voice becoming harsh

and cold. "You didn't have time to make a telephone call to your lawyer? Using a cell phone, you could have done that on your way to the airport. You didn't have time to notify the police about this important meeting? You couldn't find anyone to meet this mystery person in your place—like a law-enforcement officer, maybe?"

"I couldn't." She took one look at his cynical expression and rushed on. "She said no one around me could be trusted—even the police couldn't be trusted. She said they'd been bought."

"She?" He tilted his head and waited for her answer.

"My husband's mistress." A fresh wave of pain clenched her heart. No matter how hard she had tried, Amanda could not make her mind accept the fact that her husband had cheated on her—not sweet, kind, loving Edward. He'd never hurt her that way. But the evidence said otherwise.

Walker's expression registered surprise, and then he threw his head back and laughed. "Your husband's *mistress* called you? Aah, so now we have the motive." He placed his hands on the table and leaned closer. "Did you know the woman? Had you met her before?"

Amanda shook her head.

"Wow, let me get this straight. You expect me to believe that you received a phone call from an unknown woman identifying herself as your husband's mistress. She asked you to fly across the country for a secret meeting, and you did it? You didn't inform anyone of the call? You just jumped bail and hopped on the first plane?"

His expression darkened. His voice deepened and grew ominous. "You're either one of the stupidest women I've ever met or one of the bravest. And I'm not interested in which one." He rose abruptly and came around the table.

Oh God! I'm trying to have faith. I'm trying to believe

you are going to help me out of this mess. Please, Lord, make me stronger.

Chance Walker loosened her left cuff from the chair.

This is it. She'd run out of ideas for escape, run out of time to try and influence his decision to turn her in.

Please, Lord. I need more time.

Her rubbery legs almost refused to support her as he hauled her to her feet.

Amanda's gaze darted around the room, taking in the other diners who made no attempt to disguise their curiosity. Would one of them help her if she screamed or tried to protest? Noting the main exit door off the foyer, her eyes frantically darted in the direction of the kitchen. Should she make a mad dash for freedom? Would the servers let her pass, or would they block her path? Did she dare try?

Walker lifted one of her hands and then the other. He must have noted her discomfort earlier with them cuffed behind her back. This time he secured the bracelets in front of her. Maybe there was a heart inside that solid, brick wall of a man after all. Too bad she didn't have the time she'd need to try and soften it.

Looping the strap of his own duffel bag around his neck, he lifted her suitcase from the floor and, wrapping his free hand around her upper arm, steered her toward the foyer.

Amanda dug in her heels. "Wait. Stop. You have to give me more time. There's a killer out there, and you're taking away my only chance to find him."

The stoic expression on his face was all she needed to know her words fell on deaf ears. With little effort, he continued to propel her forward.

Murmurs from neighboring tables grew in volume, and every eye in the room unashamedly watched the entire scene. The blood drained from her face as Walker hustled her out the front door along with the last remnants of hope she had that this man would let her go.

Chance tried to ignore the fact that Little Miss Chatterbox hadn't uttered a single word since they'd left the bed-and-breakfast. No more pleas. No more attempts to explain. No unabashed pleading looks. She just stared out the windshield of the Jeep and sat in silence.

He shot a glance her way and quickly returned his eyes to the road. He knew he should be grateful she'd stopped fighting him.

But he wasn't.

Sympathy pulled at him again. She looked so small and defeated and alone.

But then he'd remember who she was—a rich, snobby, spoiled socialite who thought the law didn't apply to her. She'd killed her husband and then jumped bail. It was his job to bring her back—and he would.

But what if she was telling the truth? What if she was innocent? What if someone else had committed the crime and was setting her up? As far-fetched an idea as it was, he knew it was possible.

Have you ever turned in an innocent person?

Her question burned in his mind. No. He'd never turned in an innocent person.

The harder question would have been could he ever let a person he believed innocent go free?

He'd come close once. His stomach twisted, and a foul taste of bile coated his mouth as his thoughts turned to Roberta Thompson—rich, powerful, manipulative Roberta.

Chance still remembered the woman's features twisted with pain and grief as she swore that she hadn't killed her four-year-old son. She claimed the child had meant everything to her—that she didn't want to live without him.

He had allowed himself to believe the lies. He had seriously considered letting her go, pretending he hadn't found her. Sympathy made him weak and careless. It had been a mistake—an almost fatal one. Absently, he rubbed a hand across the left side of his chest and pictured the puckered scar where the bullet had entered. A couple of centimeters over and he wouldn't be here today.

But he had survived. Now, here he was again, falling for convincing lies and feeling sorry for another "innocent" person.

He sighed heavily as he pulled the Jeep off the road and drove toward a large storagelike building. He washed a hand over his weary face. He couldn't wait to get out of this business. His emotions were starting to rule his head. His experience with Roberta taught him that lesson loud and clear. She hadn't been innocent and neither was Mrs. Amanda Stowe.

"Where are we?" She spoke for the first time since he'd put her in the vehicle.

"Art Trenton has been gracious enough to arrange for your transportation back. You remember him, don't you? He's the bail bondsman you stiffed when you ran."

Amanda grimaced and lowered her head.

Chance came around the front of the car, opened the passenger door and helped her out. Without releasing his grasp on her cuffs, he opened the rear door, pulled the bags out and dropped them on the ground.

A man exited the building and hurried toward them.

"Mr. Walker?" He offered Chance his hand. "I'm Santana, your pilot."

Chance shook his hand and glanced over the man's shoulder.

Santana glanced back, as well. "Don't worry. The plane's right in front of this hangar and ready to go. Why don't you take your prisoner around front and I'll grab these bags?"

Prisoner. Chance glanced into the misty brown eyes looking up at him. At this moment, she looked like anything but a prisoner. He shook his head in the hope he'd knock some sense into it and, still clutching the cuffs, led her around the hangar. He was almost to the plane when Amanda dug her feet in the snow and stopped walking.

"What's that? You're not putting me on that." Her face had lost all color.

Chance looked at the high-winged, twin engine Cessna. The door stood ajar revealing the four seats within—pilot, copilot and a small bench seat for two.

"That plane is your ticket home. And, yes, I am definitely putting you on it." Chance had to drag her to the steps. "Get in."

"I can't." She grasped his coat. "I'm terrified of heights."

"You flew here, didn't you?" he asked.

"Yes, in a plane…a big, huge, heavily populated jet… not in a tin can with wheels. I was scared to death on a jet that was a hundred times the size of this." She glanced inside the Cessna and then back at Chance. "You don't understand. I can't climb in there. I'll never survive the trip."

Chance grinned. "Now there's the manipulative, conniving girl I've grown to know. For a minute, I actually believed you'd given up. I'll hand it to you. This is a new twist. I must admit it's a refreshing break from the 'I'm innocent' routine."

"I'm not kidding. This isn't a ruse, Mr. Walker. Please. I'm terrified of heights. I can't get in there." She glanced inside the open doorway and then faced him. "I'll do anything you say," she said. "Please, I'm begging you. Can't we wait a little longer and go back on a bigger plane?" Her breathing came fast and furious. "What's an extra hour or two?"

Santana stepped past them and threw their bags in the back of the plane. "Mr. Trenton already paid for this flight. I'm not giving him a refund if you decide to split."

Amanda stepped closer to Chance. The light floral scent on her skin teased his senses. She clutched his coat tighter. Her eyes wide, her expression panicked. For an instant she reminded him of a wild horse thrashing around a corral trying to avoid the saddle.

Maybe she was right. What harm could it do to switch to a bigger plane? If she kept her promise and stopped trying to cajole him into letting her go, the peace and quiet might be worth the short delay.

"Bounty hunters get paid a flat fee, don't they?" She looked up into his face. "I'll double it. Triple it. Name your price. Just don't put me on that plane."

Her words hit him like a pail of ice water. And to think he almost fell for it—again. What was he thinking? Hadn't he learned that spoiled little rich girls believed money could buy anything—anyone? Well, it couldn't buy him.

"Get in."

"No." She hit him with her fists. She tried to drop to the ground.

Chance wrapped his arm around her waist and pulled her against him, half lifting, half carrying her. He plopped her onto the bench seat, climbed in beside her and closed the door.

The pilot, already settled into his seat, donned his headset and started the engine.

Amanda looked at Chance, her face wet with tears, her skin white as snow.

This wasn't an act. This woman was scared half out of her mind. Would it kill him to drive into Fairbanks and grab a larger plane? Before he could react, the floor shifted beneath him throwing him against the back of the bench seat.

"Buckle up and put on your headsets," Santana yelled over his shoulder as he taxied onto the short runway.

"Wait." Chance righted himself and hurriedly donned his headset so he could speak to the pilot. "Stop. We're going to take another plane."

"Sorry, buddy. Why don't you fix her a stiff drink and knock her out?" Santana leaned his arm back and tried to hand him a flask.

Chance threw a disapproving glare at the pilot and ignored his offer. Realizing it was too late to change the situation, he buckled Amanda's seat belt and placed a headset on her head so they could communicate. Then he fastened his own seat belt. Her stillness frightened him. She stared into space, her eyes so wide they seemed to fill her whole face. Her breathing was nothing more than short, hiccup-like breaths.

A wave of guilt washed over him.

He patted her hand, feeling compelled to comfort her and not having a clue how.

As the plane climbed and banked sharply to the left, Amanda opened her mouth wide and screamed. The piercing, terrified sound filled the headsets and almost broke his eardrum.

A string of curses came from the pilot. "Shut her up."

The plane continued to climb and then banked sharply a second time. The sky tilted, and the ground beneath them came into sharp focus.

Amanda glanced out of the window and panicked. She turned and threw herself against Chance's arm, burying her face in his coat, clinging to him in desperation.

* * *

A man stepped out of the hangar and watched the small Cessna straighten out and then disappear on the horizon. He lifted a cell phone from his pocket and dialed. When his call was answered, he said simply, "It's done."

THREE

"Turn the plane around," Chance ordered.

"What?" The pilot glanced over his shoulder, pretending not to have heard although the headsets worked just fine.

"We have to go back." Chance frowned as he reached out to swipe Amanda's hair back from her face. Perspiration coated her forehead, and her glazed eyes stared unseeingly at him.

Unless she was rehearsing for an Academy Award, this was no act. She was going into shock. He should have listened to her. He could see how frightened she'd been before they left. But when she'd tried to buy her way out of the situation, he allowed his pride and his past experiences to cloud his judgment.

"Santana, are you deaf?" Chance yelled into his mouthpiece. "I told you to turn this tin can around. I'll drive into Fairbanks, and we'll take a commercial flight back to D.C."

"No way, buddy. I'm not giving up my fee. I got a hefty piece of change to make this run."

Chance stared at the man incredulously. "What's the matter with you? Can't you see this woman is terrified?"

Santana glanced over his shoulder at Amanda and grinned. "I told you to use the booze and knock her out."

He reached down beside his seat and pulled out the flask. "Change your mind?"

"Why you…" Chance released his seat belt and started to lean forward.

Santana raised the nose of the plane and threw Chance against the back of the seat. "Don't try that again, mister. I'm not turning the plane around. So you better figure out a way to keep your prisoner quiet. She's breaking my eardrums. Unplug her headphones."

Amanda clasped Chance's wrist in a death grip. "I'm going to be sick." Her words came out in staccato whispers as though she was fighting nausea with each one.

The pilot nodded toward the pocket on the back of the empty copilot seat. "Barf bags are right in front of you. And hurry up. I'm charging extra if she messes up my upholstery."

Chance pulled out the bag and placed it on Amanda's lap. "You need to calm down, Amanda. Take deep breaths in through your nose and blow out slowly through pursed lips. Maybe that will help."

He felt like a heel. Who was he kidding? He was a heel. He could have taken her to Fairbanks. Why did he have to let his male pride get in the way? One word entered his mind. Roberta. Chance was so determined not to repeat his mistake that he turned a blind eye to the genuine terror in Amanda's eyes.

Amanda.

Uh-oh. When had he stopped thinking of her as Mrs. Stowe: prisoner and murderer?

Amanda bowed at the waist clinging to the bag like a lifeline but so far not using it.

"Do you have any water on board?" Chance almost spat the words into his headset. He wanted to shake Santana within an inch of his life. This wasn't the time or place. But once they landed…

"There's a cooler behind your seat. Water's in there."

Chance retrieved a cold bottle from the cooler and offered it to Amanda. "Here. Maybe this will make you feel a little better, but sip it slowly."

Her trembling fingers reached for the bottle. Chance winced inwardly as his eyes fell on the chafed skin beneath the cuffs on her wrists. Maybe he should release the cuffs. It wasn't like she was going anywhere. But after a moment's consideration, he stayed firm. Regulations required he leave them on. He glanced again at the cuffs and then turned his head away. She was a prisoner, not a waiflike woman who needed his help. Prisoner. Prisoner. Prisoner. Why wouldn't the word sear itself into his mind?

Amanda glanced up. Her eyes widened as she looked out the window and a moan like the whining of a wounded animal filled their headsets.

"Man, can't you make her cut it out?" Santana asked. "I'm cutting off her headset if you can't keep her quiet."

Chance sucked in a breath. It took every ounce of control not to wrap his hands around the man's throat and squeeze the life out of him. It was obvious that they were at the pilot's mercy. But that would not last forever and then he'd teach the man a much needed lesson on how to treat people. Anticipation brought a grim smile to his face.

He took one look at the sick, scared woman beside him and felt helpless.

It was a feeling he didn't experience often and one he didn't like. He had to distract her, get her mind off of the flight. Maybe if he could talk her into closing her eyes. No, the sensation of moving would probably be worse with her eyes closed. But if she kept looking out the window at the ground below, he wasn't sure how ill she'd really become.

An idea popped into his head. He twisted and contorted until he could pull her suitcase toward their seat. He grinned with satisfaction as he slid open the front zippered compartment, slid his hand inside and grasped the object he sought.

Amanda's eyes looked empty, weary. She made no effort to speak and just stared at him.

"Here. Maybe this will help." Chance placed her Bible in her hands.

A ghost of a smile touched Amanda's lips as she clasped the book on her lap.

"Thank you," she whispered.

A glistening pool of tears in her eyes reached right into his chest and squeezed the breath out of him. He'd never been affected by tears before and he'd seen plenty from male and female alike in his line of work. But there was something different—something special, almost vulnerable and innocent about Amanda.

She opened the book, her fingers tracing a path line by line across the page.

Chance watched in amazement as the more she read the calmer she became. Her lips moved ever so slightly. Remembering how she'd behaved at breakfast he assumed she was praying. He was grateful this time she did it silently but even more grateful it seemed to be working.

A short time later, Amanda's breathing returned to normal. She never took her eyes off the pages, and her lips never stopped their silent movement. But at least she seemed a thousand percent calmer.

He didn't understand how a mere book could make such a marked difference in a person. It was brainwashing if you asked him. But at this moment he didn't care what she was reading. It worked. That was all that mattered.

Daring to relax for the first time since the plane took

off, Chance stole a moment to enjoy the view. The snow-covered mountains stretched before him like white caps in a stormy sea. He had to admit it was difficult to experience the wonders of nature and not believe in something beyond the stupidity and frailty of man. It wasn't that he didn't believe in a higher power. As a kid, he'd never been taught to believe or disbelieve.

But he'd witnessed many churchgoing people do cruel things, break laws, break hearts. Whatever they read in that Bible sure didn't seem to rub off in their day-to-day lives. Nope. It was not for him.

Tension seeped out of his muscles. He hadn't realized how stressed he'd been over the past hour. He dared to relax and watched the plane's shadow cross the peaks beneath him. Evergreen trees cloaked the mountains like emerald robes. The magnificence took his breath away. Maybe this trip wouldn't be so bad after all.

A subtle awareness crept into his consciousness. Chance straightened his shoulders and sat up straight. He drew in a deep breath. After a moment, he tilted his head and inhaled again.

"What's that smell?" he asked Santana.

"I don't smell anything."

"Take a whiff. What is that?"

The pilot grumbled beneath his breath but did what Chance asked.

Alarm slithered down Chance's spine. His eyes shot to the pilot's and he knew by the man's sudden paleness that they both recognized the scent.

Smoke!

"Do you see anything?" Chance purposely kept his tone of voice calm and he avoided the word *fire,* not wanting to upset Amanda again.

"No. You?" The man wasn't so cocky now as he

checked and double-checked the instruments on the control panel. He stared a bit longer at one gauge and then said, "Look behind us. Do you see any vapors?"

Vapors? Gasoline. Santana thinks we have a fuel leak.

Because the Cessna was a high-wing plane it was almost impossible to be sure, but after careful scrutiny, Chance didn't think they were trailing any vapors. "No. Nothing."

He glanced at Amanda. She kept her eyes glued to her Bible. Her lips moved faster, and her prayers had escalated from silent lip movements to barely audible murmurs. Otherwise she showed no signs of being aware there was anything out of the ordinary going on.

A string of curses poured out of Santana's mouth. "Fuel's spraying my feet. The manifold is hot. We have a fuel leak in the engine compartment."

"What do we do?"

"We get on the ground. Fast."

The plane dipped forward almost as quickly as Santana had spoken as he forced the plane to lose altitude.

Amanda's knuckles whitened as she grasped her Bible, but otherwise she didn't show any signs of panic.

Whether there was a God or not, Chance was grateful that *she* believed there was one. A sick, screaming woman was the last thing he needed on his hands at the moment.

The plane's speed of descent increased and forced both Amanda and Chance against the back of their seat. He placed a hand on her arm. "It's going to be okay, Mrs. Stowe. Don't look up. Just keep reading your book." He hadn't needed to offer that suggestion; her eyes never strayed from the book in her lap.

A string of curses again filled their headphones. "We've lost communication with the ground. The wires must be fried."

Whispers of a light, white smoke twirled around Santana's feet. The white-gray mist covered his shoes and then moved like an ominous snake coursing its away along the floor of the plane.

Chance clamped his jaw tight. The ground was coming up fast, no more than a couple hundred feet below. He could see the top of the mountains looming closer. It was what he saw out the plane's windshield that caused him to suck in a deep breath.

Trees.

No runway or lake or open field.

Just hundreds of evergreen trees poking out of the snow.

Suddenly Chance wished he could offer a silent prayer of his own to Amanda's God. A lead weight seized his stomach, and every muscle in his body shook as the plane vibrated and tossed about in the air currents as it continued to descend.

Amanda reached over and placed her hand on his forearm. When he turned his head to look at her, a gentle, sweet smile graced her face.

"Don't die without knowing Jesus, Mr. Walker. Close your eyes and ask Him into your heart."

Chance closed his eyes—not because he wanted to ask an imaginary being into his heart but because he didn't want to get glass in his eyes when sixty seconds from now they crashed.

Trapped in a current of wind, the plane bounced violently. Unable to resist, Chance reopened his eyes and stared out the windshield. He still didn't see anything resembling a flat surface.

Fear twisted his insides into a painful knot when he realized what Santana was going to attempt. He was going to try to land between the trees.

Seconds ticked by as they continued to lose altitude, and then they hit.

Everything seemed to be happening in slow motion.

The screeching, earsplitting sound of crushing metal pierced his ears as they plowed through trees that clawed at the plane and ripped the wings off.

The force of the impact whiplashed him forward and then backward. The seat belt squeezed his chest like a vise, making it impossible to draw a deep breath.

The fuselage bounced and bucked like a bull in a rodeo as it skidded across the ground. Every item not bolted down flew through the air, and more than one object slammed into Chance's head. Logically he knew it had only been seconds, but it felt like an eternity. Weren't they ever going to stop?

And then he saw it.

It was a large tree trunk looming in front of them like a giant, impenetrable wall.

It grew larger with every passing second.

"Mr. Walker…"

Amanda's voice whispering his name was the last sound he heard.

FOUR

Amanda tried to open her eyes, but her lids felt like they had fifty-pound weights holding them down. She paused to clear the fog in her head and get her bearings. Then she tried again. A sliver of light seeped in beneath the narrow openings but was followed by a jolt of pain so intense that it forced her to grit her teeth and squeeze her eyes shut tight.

What's happened to me?

She winced. Boy, did she have a granddaddy of headaches.

Something sharp was cutting into her ribs. Her twisted body made it feel like she was suspended in air.

What was going on?

Frustrated and confused, she turned to her side and tried to sit up. A burst of white-hot light exploded behind her eyelids and brought tears to her eyes when she tried to move.

Okay. No sitting up.

Maybe she should just lie still until she could figure it all out. She forced herself to breath slowly—in, out.

As the seconds slid by, Amanda's other senses took over. She became aware of a strong, acrid smell of smoke. Waves of frigid air brushed across her face burning her cheeks and nose. She must be outside somewhere. But where? Had she been hit by a car? It sure felt like it.

Oh Lord, why can't I open my eyes?

Then she became aware of another sensation—the taste of blood pooling in her mouth, dribbling down her chin. Her pulse raced with fear.

"Mrs. Stowe? Can you hear me?"

She recognized the deep male voice but couldn't place a face or name to it.

Strong hands gently lifted her from her uncomfortable perch and placed her on a solid, flat surface.

"Let me get you out of these cuffs."

Cuffs?

Memory flooded back with the force of water spewing from a broken dam.

Cuffs. Chance Walker, bounty hunter. Amanda Stowe, prisoner.

Oh God, help me. She remembered now.

The sound of metal clinking against metal and the liberating sensation of freed wrists spurred her into action. Seized by a wave of panic, she ignored the pain, forced her eyes open and tried to sit up.

"Whoa, hold on. Take your time. You've taken a nasty bump to your head. You might have a concussion."

Amanda did as she was told and tried something really simple—like blinking. Something wet and sticky prevented her left eye from opening more than a slit. But after a blink or two, she could open her right eye. When she was finally able to focus, Chance Walker came into view. The worried expression on his face almost fooled her into thinking he actually cared that she was injured. But of course, he cared—no prisoner, no money.

She took a good look at Chance, and the damage to his face made her catch her breath. Deep gashes sliced through his forehead and cheek. Mottled skin surrounding both eyes made him look like he'd gone ten rounds in a boxing match—and lost. If he looked this bad now, Amanda could only imagine how much worse he'd look tomorrow when the bruising would be more evident.

"You're hurt." Her instinct was to reach out her hand and offer comfort. Her mind stilled that action. She wouldn't touch an injured snake without expecting to be bitten, would she?

"I'm fine." He brushed off her concern and continued to stare at her.

Blood filled her mouth and made talking difficult. Had she lost a tooth? Bitten her tongue? She turned her head and spit before saying, "You don't look fine."

"It's worse for you than me. You have to look at me." His grin twisted his features into a live horror mask, and she didn't know whether to laugh or cry. *Oh Heavenly Father, help us. He's been so badly injured.*

Chance clasped her shoulders and eased her against a hard surface giving support to her back. Amanda looked around her and wished she hadn't.

The plane, or what little was left of it, resembled crumpled and discarded aluminum foil. The wings were gone. Half the roof was gone, and huge evergreen limbs were imbedded where the missing pieces of the roof had been.

The plane must have split in half upon impact since nothing but a large gaping hole filled the space where the back of the plane had been.

Looking through that same hole, she could see the missing parts of the plane in the distance. The back of the plane had imbedded itself in the ground, the tail up in the air and the wreckage leaning precariously to the right. She couldn't believe it. She'd always been terrified of flying. Now her worst fears had come true. Her plane had crashed.

But maybe now she could remove it from her top ten terrors list—after all, it had happened and yet she'd survived.

See, Lord. I knew I was always afraid of heights for a reason. If you had intended us to fly you would have given us wings. How come I'm the only one who knows that?

"Help me." The panic in Mr. Santana's voice caught her attention. "Get me out of here."

Chance turned and dug through several items that had come loose during the crash in an attempt to gain clear access to the pilot. Amanda crawled beside him. When they had an unobstructed view of the situation, they glanced at each other in horror. The plane's engine and control panel had come forward and now pinned the pilot's legs beneath it.

"Hold on, Santana. Let me get a good look at the situation," Chance said.

Amanda watched as Chance tried to slide his hand between the top of the man's leg and the wreckage pinning him. Santana screamed out in pain and then followed up with a stream of expletives. Chance tried to squeeze behind the man's seat. Hooking his hands under his arms, he slowly tried to tug him out. Santana screamed again.

Dropping to his belly, Chance crawled forward and braced his shoulder and part of his back under a piece of the wreckage on top of Santana. His face turned red with the effort to lift it enough for the pilot to wriggle free, but the metal wouldn't budge.

"I can't feel my legs." The fear in his voice became full-blown panic and the pilot screamed, "Get me out of here!"

The terror in his voice stirred Amanda's heart. She shifted her body closer and placed a hand on his shoulder. "Please, Mr. Santana. Don't panic. We'll get you out. But you've got to control yourself. Panicking will only make things worse."

"We need to radio the control tower for help," Chance said.

The pilot pushed against the U-shaped steering wheel biting into his gut and tried again to pull his legs loose but failed. "We lost all communication before the crash. Remember?" Then he peppered the air again with foul language.

"Enough already, Santana," Chance commanded. "The situation's bad enough without having to listen to that garbage. I can't hear myself think. If you want my help then shut up."

Amanda ducked her head and remained silent. Although grateful that the foul tirade ceased, Chance's method wasn't exactly how she would have liked to see the situation handled. Obviously, the man was scared. So was she.

"Mr. Santana. Someone will find us." She tried to keep her voice soft and soothing. "We have to keep a positive attitude and do the best we can to stay safe and warm while we wait for help to come. Would you like to say a prayer with me? Maybe it will bring you some comfort."

Santana's face reddened. He opened his mouth to yell something at Amanda—more foul language, no doubt—but one censoring glance from the bounty hunter silenced him, and he turned his head away.

"Mrs. Stowe, I'm going to need your help." Chance Walker hovered over her. "How are you feeling? Can you stand up?"

Her head throbbed and she still couldn't open her left eye more than a slit, but all in all she thought she should be able to stand. Chance Walker offered his arm. Amanda reached out, grateful for the strength in his forearm as she pulled herself to an upright position.

The situation seemed so surreal. Bent and twisted fu-

selage came about chest high, but she was able to stand
up straight because the plane had no roof, a piece of metal
here or there, a broken tree limb or two tangled in the
wreckage but nothing of substance.

"You okay?" Chance's eyes bored into her, his forearm
still steadying her.

"Yes."

"Are you sure?"

Amanda nodded.

"Good. We have to prepare to stay the night just in case
help doesn't come right away. We'll need to check and see
what supplies we have. We'll need to fortify the plane for
shelter. We'll need heat. Food." He took a deep breath and
stared into her eyes. "Can I count on you?"

Count on her? For what? To not remember that she was
his prisoner? Not try to escape the first opportunity she
had? One sarcastic retort after another flooded her mind,
but instead she simply nodded.

"We need to locate our luggage and anything else of
use that we can find." He glanced at the wreckage located in the distance. "I hope the luggage managed to stay
inside and wasn't strewn for miles. The roof looks intact
from here, so if the sides stayed intact too maybe we'll be
lucky."

Amanda followed the direction of his gaze. What if
the luggage wasn't still on board? The thought of hiking
through these woods looking for damaged luggage and
strewn contents made her stomach clench.

"I'm freezing." Despite the heavy winter coat he wore,
Santana's arms wrapped around his upper torso and his
teeth chattered. He shifted and squirmed again in an attempt to free himself but swallowed whatever retort he
might have made when he failed to move.

Chance removed his coat and tucked it around Santana's body. "Here. This should help until I get a fire going and find out what supplies we have left."

"What about you?" Amanda whispered as he passed her.

"I've got on thermal underwear, a flannel shirt and a wool sweater. It'll do for now. Let's hurry."

Without a word passing between them, they hiked several hundred yards to the rest of the plane. When they arrived, they saw one whole side of the plane had been ripped away. Rummaging through the tree limbs and debris of what was left, they located a first aid kit, a flashlight, a couple of blankets and the pilot's small emergency supply bag.

Amanda didn't see her suitcase anywhere. It must have been thrown from the wreckage during the crash. She found Chance's duffel bag wedged beneath a metal fold in the plane's hull. It was open and upside down but looked like most of the contents were still inside.

Together they gathered everything they could and dragged it through the woods and back to the cockpit shell.

Chance immediately reached inside his duffel bag, extracting both a knife and a small ax. He pulled the knife free from its sheath. Amanda's eyes widened at the sight of the long blade with the sharp, serrated edges at the tip.

"What are you going to use that for?" she asked.

"Protection. We are surrounded by wildlife, Mrs. Stowe—wildlife that might want our company tonight."

Amanda glanced into the woods. "What kind of…?" Her breath hitched in her throat as her mind envisioned coming face-to-face with a grizzly bear. "Are there grizzly bears out here?" She could barely get the words out of her mouth, and she processed the fact that a tiny ax and a hunter's knife would not be protection against them.

"Bears are in hibernation at this time of year. Not that

they can't be awakened so I wouldn't wander out on my own if I was you. If you think I'm dangerous, try coming face-to-face with a grumpy bear you just woke up."

He threw a glance over his shoulder as he bent to gather more supplies and grinned that rakish, dangerous grin that mesmerized her. "I was thinking more along the lines of wolves. Food is scarce this time of year, and they might consider us dinner dropped into their laps."

Amanda couldn't stop her eyes from widening, but she made an effort to make sure she didn't show any other signs of the fear crawling up and down her spine.

Chance chuckled, held the knife up higher, the blade gleaming in the sunlight. "Speaking of food, this might come in pretty handy, as well. All I have in my duffel bag is a package of dried fruit and a half-dozen granola bars." He nodded at the supply bag at her feet. "Let's hope you'll find a couple of days' rations tucked inside the pilot's emergency case."

"But for now, I'm going to cut off some of the smaller evergreen branches. Winters in Alaska have subzero temperatures. If we are going to survive the night, I'll have to rig something for shelter. I'm going to need you to go through that bag and see what we can use. When you're finished, I could also use some help gathering all the sticks and any dry grass you can find for a fire."

Santana snorted a laugh and took a long pull from the flask he'd had tucked by his seat. "You're a regular Boy Scout, aren't you?"

Chance glared at the man. "For your sake, you better hope I am." He nodded at the flask. "Alcohol lowers your core body temperature. I wouldn't continue drinking that if I were you."

"Yeah, well lucky for me I'm not you." He took another drag.

Chance muttered a sound of disgust and walked off into the woods.

Momentary panic seized Amanda the minute he disappeared from sight. What if he got hurt? Or lost? What if he didn't come back? From the moment she'd met him, she had fantasized a million ways to make him disappear. Now the thought that he might not return scared her to death. Forcing herself to stay in control of her emotions, she began searching the bags.

Chance's hands ached. The frigid air had stiffened his joints and made it difficult to bend his fingers. He needed to get back. Soon. For once, he was grateful he had recently put on a few extra pounds. He needed every extra inch of belt he could muster as he removed it from his waist and wrapped it around the base of the limbs. Pulling the bundled pile of evergreen limbs behind him, he cradled as many additional limbs as he could carry against his body and moved forward. The weight of the tree limbs combined with the lack of air in this high altitude sapped his energy and made it difficult to breathe.

Even though he'd only wandered a few hundred feet from the wreckage, fighting his way back through the brush was no picnic. His nose and cheeks throbbed from the biting cold. The temperature must have dropped at least ten degrees over the past hour. Tree branches slapped and stung his face.

Chance glanced up at the sun. They had a few good hours of daylight left. Precious few. If he had to be stranded in the Alaskan wilderness, why couldn't it have been in summer when daylight seemed endless and berries and wildlife were plentiful?

No such luck. It was the middle of December, and snow covered the ground. If he had to hazard a guess, he'd say it probably hadn't even made double digits right now with nowhere to go but down. He hoped these evergreens would help insulate the shell of the plane enough to help them make it through the night without freezing to death. That thought alone made him walk faster.

Thank God they were still alive.

God?

It was just a saying, he reminded himself. Everybody said it at one time or another. It didn't mean a thing. Right? Half a day with Amanda and she already had him entertaining the possibility that God might really exist.

Amanda?

He meant prisoner Stowe. He repeated the words over and over in his mind until he was able to think of her as just that—prisoner Stowe and nothing more. He tried to ignore how her vulnerability and fear pushed all his protective buttons.

Suddenly, a finger of dread crept up his spine.

He'd removed her handcuffs and left her alone at the wreckage. She wouldn't think this was an opportunity to try and escape, would she? She'd have to realize she couldn't survive on her own. She didn't have the proper clothing, equipment or food. No matter how desperate she was to get away, she wouldn't be stupid enough to take off in these woods without a weapon, would she? He idly patted the gun in his shoulder harness, reassuring himself it was still there. Then he remembered the small ax he'd left behind.

If she'd taken off, he'd have to go after her—not because of the sizable finder's fee he'd lose if she got away but because she was his responsibility. She had been from the moment he'd put her on the plane. She'd be committing suicide trying to make it out of this wilderness alone, and he couldn't let that happen.

He lowered his head and shoulders, pushing through the brush and thicket like a defensive end on a football field. Nothing was going to stop him. Within minutes, he'd reached a small clearing, the wreckage only a few yards ahead.

He paused for a moment.

Silence.

There shouldn't be silence. He should hear Amanda and the pilot talking. He should hear Amanda rummaging through the luggage. He should see her moving about the fuselage.

But the deathly, silent stillness twisted his insides.

She was gone!

He dropped the branches and covered the few dozen yards in seconds.

Although the roof was missing, he still had to bend his head to pass beneath the tree limbs the plane had ripped and dragged with their descent. He shot a look to the front of the plane and saw Amanda.

She sat on the floor, her back against the controls, her knees bent, her right shoulder leaning heavily against the pilot. She didn't speak when she saw him, but her eyes did the talking for her. She looked terrified.

"Amanda?" An uneasy feeling crawled up Chance's spine.

"It's about time you got back." The pilot's slurred speech confirmed Chance's suspicion that he had ignored his order to put the flask away.

"The little missy and I were beginning to think you'd taken off and left us."

"What's going on?" Chance demanded. "Amanda, are you okay?"

"She's fine…for now." The pilot threw a glance over

his shoulder. "And if you want your prisoner to stay that way then you'll do exactly as I say."

"Mr. Walker…" Amanda started to get up, and the pilot tightened his grip on her upper arm and pulled her back against him.

"Anh, Anh, Anh. You know better than that lady. Stay put."

"Take your hands off of her." Chance glared at him and tried to control his rage. Injured or not, this man needed someone to teach him a lesson in how to be a human being.

"Okay, okay. Don't get yourself all bent out of shape." The pilot grinned at Chance. "But first remove that gun from your shoulder holster. Nice and slow if you please. Slide the gun and that big ugly knife you have over here to me."

Chance frowned and stared back at Santana. "Not on your life."

"Oh, no. Not on my life." Santana raised his right hand and held a twenty-two caliber pistol against Amanda's chest. "On hers."

FIVE

"Let's talk about this." Chance tried to keep his voice calm and nonthreatening. Slowly, he stepped forward.

"There's nothing to talk about." Santana pushed his weapon harder against Amanda's chest.

Chance grimaced when Amanda winced.

"I'm pinned down in this pile of tin cans," Santana said. "And there's no way I'm gonna let the two of you take off and leave me behind."

"No one is leaving you." Chance inched closer.

"Well, that's nice of you to say, Mr. Boy Scout, but give me your weapons. Then I'll be sure that you're telling the truth."

"Mr. Walker, please do what he says," Amanda begged.

One look into the pilot's wild, inebriated eyes and Chance knew there'd be no reasoning with him. Slowly, he released his sidearm, placed it and his knife down and slid it as requested.

Santana released his hold on her arm as he scooped up the discarded weapons.

Amanda didn't waste the opportunity to get away from the pilot and moved away as quickly as possible. Within seconds, Chance had grabbed her arm and placed her safely behind him.

"Now what?" Chance asked, his eyes never leaving the gun in Santana's hand.

"Now go about your business," Santana said. "You're not going anywhere without weapons so do what you want." He tipped back his head and emptied the rest of his flask.

Chance watched the pilot stretch his left arm behind his seat and withdraw a second flask from a belly bag strapped to the seat.

"Haven't you had enough?" Chance growled. "That stuff's going to kill you."

"Mind your own business. Your legs aren't pinned. I need a drink or two."

Chance shook his head, made a sound of disgust and turned away.

"What are we going to do now?" Amanda whispered.

"He's going to kill himself drinking alcohol in these temperatures. But that's his choice. We're going to build a shelter so we don't die of hypothermia, too."

Amanda's teeth chattered so hard her teeth hurt—whether from the cold or as an aftereffect of the past few hours of life-threatening, nonstop stress, she wasn't sure. She'd been captured by a bounty hunter, survived an airplane crash, been held at gunpoint by a drunken pilot and was trapped in the Alaskan wilderness with a bad guy and worse guy as companions. What else could go wrong? She had to admit she didn't want to know.

She noted Chance's red nose and cheeks as well as a slight bluish tinge to his lips. Together with the swelling and bruising he'd sustained in the crash, Amanda couldn't help but wonder if even his mother would recognize such a horribly damaged face. "You're freezing. You need to take your coat back."

"I'm fine."

"You're not fine."

Chance ignored her and started to poke through the items she'd retrieved from the baggage and had placed on the floor of the plane.

"Hey!" Amanda grabbed Chance's sleeve and made him stop what he was doing to look at her. "You're one step away from freezing to death. You need to take your coat back from the pilot. We brought blankets back with us from the wreckage. We can wrap one of them around Santana. He's wearing his own coat and only using yours as a blanket anyway. You're the one doing the work around here. You need your coat."

Chance seemed surprised at her outburst. "Why, darlin', I didn't think you cared."

"I don't."

He wore the same rakish grin he'd flashed at their breakfast table. Had it only been a short time ago they were staring each other down and fighting over whether she wanted eggs or pancakes? The whole situation seemed surreal.

"Are you sure?" His grin widened.

Amanda planted her hands on her hips and locked her eyes with his. "Not for any of the reasons racing around in your caveman mind. But if you think I'm going to let both of you crazy, foolish men kill yourselves and strand me alone up here, guess again."

She reached over and grabbed a blanket from the floor. "Here. Go get your coat back. I'd do it, but I'm not too fond of having the barrel of a gun shoved into my chest."

Chance chuckled, accepted the blanket from her hand and moved toward the pilot. A few moments later, the reluctant pilot, now burrowed beneath a heavy woolen blanket, had relinquished the borrowed coat.

Besides the woolen blankets, Amanda hadn't found much inside the pilot's emergency bag—a tarp, a couple of flares, two silver survival blankets and a single sleeping bag. A quick search inside Chance's duffel bag didn't fare much better—three granola bars, a bottle of water, a small package of dried fruit, a couple of tea-light candles and a pack of waterproof matches.

She presented them to him now. "I must admit I found it intriguing that a bounty hunter would travel with tea lights in his knapsack."

"In a few seconds, you're going to be very happy I have those candles." Chance replied. "Can you gather some kindling while I throw up this tarp and start building a shelter?"

Santana waved his gun. "Neither of you are going anywhere."

Amanda didn't know if Chance's scowl had the desired effect on the pilot, but it was lethal enough to stop her dead in her tracks.

"You're a fool, Santana. Do you really believe she's going to take off with no weapons or supplies?"

"She's a prisoner, isn't she? If I had a choice between facing a life sentence because I stayed put or taking my chances on escaping and being free, I know which one I'd pick."

"The woman isn't stupid. She knows she'd never stand a chance of surviving if she took off." Chance's attention immediately shifted to Amanda, and their eyes locked. "Isn't that right?"

She wanted to give that pilot a good, swift kick. Every time she took one step forward in gaining this bounty hunter's trust, something would happen to send her three steps back. At this rate, how was she ever going to get him to listen to her side of the story?

Even though Chance's words expressed confidence in her, it was evident the pilot had planted another seed of doubt in his mind. He wasn't looking at her now as he had a few moments ago. She wasn't a woman stranded with him in the wilderness anymore. A partner working to survive? No. His dark, wary eyes bored into her. Silently warning her not to even think of trying to run away. A few carelessly spoken words from the pilot and he no longer looked at her as anything than what she'd been to him from the beginning—Mrs. Stowe, prisoner.

Amanda looked him straight in the eye and said, "When the two of you Neanderthals fall asleep, I intend to steal your weapons and supplies. That's when you'll have to worry about me but not before."

Chance's eyes widened with surprise, and then he laughed. "Thanks for the warning. I'm shaking in my boots." He threw a look back at the pilot. "She's going for dry wood, and I'm building a shelter out of this wreckage. If you want to shoot us and sign your own death warrant then go ahead and shoot."

Slowly, he turned his back on Santana and began opening the tarp.

The pilot stared at Amanda, indecision written all over his face. Muttering under his breath, he lowered the weapon.

"Well?"

Fear crawled up Jeff "Lucky" Lupine's spine at the rigid, unforgiving tone in the voice on the other end of the phone, and he wasn't one to scare easily.

"Everything went exactly as planned," Lucky hurried to assure his boss. "The plane never arrived at the designated landing site. I figure it went down in the mountains."

"You figure? You don't know?"

The words held an unspoken lethal threat.

"Look, I sliced the fuel lines. The vibration of the plane should have been enough to break the line the rest of the way. And I checked. They never made it to our meeting place. So I'm certain they crashed. They were in the middle of nowhere. No place to land. Nothing but mountains and trees. They couldn't have survived a crash. No way."

"And you know this because…?"

The barely controlled, steel coldness of the other man's voice made Lucky break out in a sweat despite the freezing temperatures.

"Look, boss, even if they did survive a crash, they'll never find their way back. It's pure wilderness for hundreds of miles, and these are city folks. They'll get mauled by an animal or freeze to death or starve. Don't worry. If they're not dead yet they're going to be soon…real soon."

"I certainly hope so—for your sake. Or they won't be the only ones."

Lucky clenched the phone receiver in his hand. He wasn't being paid enough to put up with this kind of treatment. But knowing what could happen to him if he shared that thought with his employer, he remained silent.

"Don't call me again until you have proof that this situation has been suitably and permanently handled. Have I made myself clear?" The voice on the other end of the line left no room for misunderstanding.

"Yes."

The gentle disconnection was more frightening than if the receiver had been slammed into the phone receptacle. His boss was not a patient man. Lucky knew he had to locate the crash site. Nothing short of three corpses would save his butt. He pulled a map from his back pocket, spread it out across the wooden table in the back of Rhoda's bar and ordered a double shot of whiskey.

How hard could it be to figure out the pilot's route? After all, he'd been the one to set up their meeting spot. He made a few notations then sat back, a satisfied smile on his lips. It was time to take his plane up for a little spin. The other plane's wreckage should be easily seen from the air if you knew where to look for it. This time he wasn't hunting bear or moose. He'd found himself entangled in a twisted "them-or-me" scenario and the only thing he knew for sure was he would be the one who would be coming back alive.

SIX

Amanda followed Chance's instructions. She didn't wander more than a few dozen yards from the fuselage, making sure she wouldn't get lost or be open prey for wildlife. She scrambled in the brush for dry twigs and dead grass, retrieving as much as she could find. When she returned, Chance had already secured the tarp as a ceiling and had laid evergreen branches on top of it for insulation.

Amanda dumped the pile on the ground. "Is this enough?"

Chance glanced at the discarded wood. "For now. Come over here and grab the end of this tarp. I need to try and form a side wall out of it."

She ducked under his arm, and suddenly the small cramped quarters seemed even smaller. The large size of his body cut off the outside cold air, and the sudden warmth made her want to burrow closer. She glanced up, and the dark intensity of his eyes made her catch her breath. Her steps faltered. Immediately he gripped her arm, his touch firm, reassuring. Emotions she didn't understand, feelings she didn't want to acknowledge caused her to panic and she pulled away from him.

"Let me go."

She almost fell as she backed away and got caught up in

the tarp. She batted her way out of it and hoped he hadn't been able to read the effect his nearness had had on her.

"Okay." He raised his left hand, his right still supporting the tarp. "Fall on your butt. See if I care. But do it after you secure the end of the tarp."

Amanda hoped the flaming heat in her cheeks would be misinterpreted as weather-related and not a blatant giveaway of how confused and unsettled she felt whenever this man drew near. She didn't know what it was about him. He was just a man like any other. Yet there was something—a pull, an awareness—that seized her emotions and messed with her senses.

Maybe it was the danger he represented. After all, he held her freedom in his hands, and at this moment he wasn't too keen on giving it back to her. And yet she didn't feel in danger when she was with him. She felt safe, protected. She forced her self-consciousness to take a backseat and watched in fascination as he quickly formed a third wall to their shelter. Bucked up by evergreen branches and naked tree limbs, the tiny new bunker presented a crude but effective barricade against the frigid air.

Amanda noted that Chance no longer had a bluish tinge to his lips. But his hands still looked raw and sore.

"Maybe you should take a break and put your hands inside your coat for a little while."

Chance glanced at the quickly setting sun. "We need to get a fire started before we lose the light. There will be time to warm them later." He squatted beside the supplies piled at his feet and rummaged through them. "Not everything's here."

Amanda looked at the items she'd retrieved from the other half of the plane wreck. "I don't understand. That's everything that was inside the bags."

"Not everything." Chance pinned her with his stare and waited as though he expected an explanation.

Did he really think she had stolen something from him? She tried to keep anger out of her voice.

"I don't know what you're asking me. Your bag was open. Maybe when I dragged it back here whatever you're missing fell out."

She pushed her hair away from her face and sat down beside him. "You're lucky your duffel bag got wedged in the wreckage. My belongings are probably strewn for miles all over the woods." She glanced over the items in the pile. "What exactly are you looking for?"

"My ax."

Now she understood. He thought she had his weapon and she was waiting for the opportunity to use it. If the idea wasn't so preposterous, she would have laughed in his face. Were all men so suspicious and mistrusting, or was it just everything-by-the-book Chance Walker? Sometimes she thought no matter what she said or did he would never trust her enough to listen to her…to not turn her in… to help her find the woman who knew the identity of her husband's murderer. That is if they ever found their way out of here in the first place.

Amanda looked him straight in the eye and answered him as honestly and calmly as possible. "I don't have your ax. If I did I would have put it in the pile with everything else."

He stared at her for a moment longer. His hesitance and suspicion made her want to pick up something and throw it at his head. But instead she forced herself not to squirm under his scrutiny and just waited for him to make up his mind if she were lying or not.

Without another word, he turned his attention back to

the items strewn on the ground, picked up the waterproof matches, a few cotton balls and one of the tea lights.

"Candles? You're actually going to light candles now?"

His lips twitched. "Watch and learn."

Chance moved through the only outside opening of their tiny shelter. He positioned the kindling a short but reasonable distance away and then shredded the cotton and tucked the smaller pieces in various positions throughout the wood.

"Santana, I need my knife." When the pilot didn't answer, Chance crawled back inside.

Santana's eyes were closed, his head lolled to one side.

"Santana." Chance jostled the man. When he got no response, he lowered his ear close to the man's mouth, waited a few seconds and then placed two fingers against the carotid artery in his neck.

The grim expression on Chance's face caused Amanda's heart to race. "Is he dead?" she whispered.

"No. But his pulse is weak." Chance lifted a half empty flask of alcohol out of his hand. "For once, I hope it's from too much alcohol and not from complications from his injuries. I'm afraid he may have some internal bleeding and if we don't get him help soon…" He didn't finish his statement. He retrieved both the guns and the knife and confiscated what was left of the alcohol. Just as he began to back away, he spotted something behind Santana's seat, reached down and brought out his small ax.

"I forgot. I gave it to him when he asked for my weapons. Sorry."

Amanda suddenly realized something else. Another piece of the puzzle regarding Chance Walker's character fell into place and she smiled.

"You could have taken those weapons from Santana at

any time. You could have overpowered him from the beginning."

Chance didn't comment as he crouched down in front of the pile of kindling.

"Why didn't you?" she asked.

He shrugged. "The man was inebriated, scared out of his mind and trapped. I imagine he was feeling pretty helpless—definitely feeling out of control of the situation. If holding on to the weapons gave him a false sense of security, I didn't see any harm in it."

Amanda tucked away this little gem of good character with all the others she'd observed since the beginning of this doomsday flight. Chance Walker was a decent man with a good heart. Now if she could only figure out a way to make him see her situation with as much empathy as he had seen the pilot's, then half her problems would be over.

Chance used the knife to liberally shave the wax from the tea light over the wood like he was seasoning a piece of meat. He struck a match and held it to the odd pieces of cotton he'd scattered throughout the kindling. He bent forward and gently blew until the cotton, wax and twigs ignited.

Amanda released the breath she hadn't been aware she'd been holding. A grin split her face. She'd never been so happy to see a campfire ignite.

"Santana was right about you," she said. "You are a regular Boy Scout."

Chance glanced in her direction and shrugged. "I did some research before I took this trip. Just in case."

Just in case? What kind of person bones up on survival tips just in case they might crash in the wilderness on their way home? Amanda lowered her head and shook it back and forth. Only a man who couldn't face failure, couldn't dare being wrong. A man who wouldn't allow himself to trust or rely on others. How was she ever going to break through his self-protective shield and convince him to trust her? And would her informant still be waiting if they ever did get out of this mess?

Sadness radiated all the way to her bones. Although she was trying not to feel anything at all—no emotions, no reactions—trying to live moment-to-moment, she had to admit she felt sorry for this bounty hunter. She couldn't imagine having no one and nothing but yourself to rely on. She couldn't fathom surviving even a day in this harsh, cruel world without being wrapped in God's love.

Amanda might be the prisoner but Chance Walker was the one who was lost.

Lucky tried not to listen to the voice in his head that urged him to turn back. He ignored the warning and kept his eyes glued on the ground below. He'd give it a few more minutes. He'd been searching for hours and hadn't seen anything. He couldn't have been wrong about the co-ordinates, could he?

Lucky eyed the AK-47 automatic weapon, the rifle and the two revolvers on the floor beside him. What had he gotten himself into? He was beginning to have doubts whether he should have agreed to take this job in the first place.

But what choice did he have? He was in too deep. Saying "no" was not an option.

"I'll give it another ten minutes," he said out loud. He checked his gauges. He was getting low on fuel. A quick glance at the sun on the horizon let him know it would be dark before he got back if he didn't turn around right now.

Fighting with himself, he decided ten more minutes couldn't hurt. He held binoculars against his eyes and continued to scan the ground below.

Twilight's shadows flitted through the trees and danced across the ground. Amanda sat cross-legged at the fire's edge. "Ahh, this feels good. I didn't realize how cold I was." She held her hands in front of her and soaked the warmth deep into her bones.

Chance acknowledged her words with a nod and tossed a couple of small, broken limbs onto the kindling. "This small amount of wood won't fuel the fire for long." He looked into the woods.

"You're not leaving, are you? It's going to be dark soon."

"I don't have a choice. I need to find your bag. As the temperature drops, you're going to need your extra clothing. And I need to chop more wood if we're going to be able to sustain the fire."

But he didn't leave right away. He continued to crouch beside the flames and warmed his hands. The only sound between them was the snapping and crackling of the fire. When he stood, he stared down at her, assessing her with his eyes. Then, as if coming to a conclusion only he could understand, he withdrew his gun.

"Do you know how to use this correctly?"

Her eyes widened and her pulse raced. "No. I don't believe in guns."

"Really? You owned one, Mrs. Stowe, remember? The one you used to shoot your husband." Before she could respond, he slid the top of the gun back and forth. "Don't point it at anything or anyone, including yourself, unless you're ready to use it. It's armed and ready to fire. Second, shoot in the middle of the greatest mass. That way you're bound to hit something."

Amanda swallowed the lump in her throat and gingerly accepted the weapon with the same enthusiasm as if he were handing her a sleeping snake.

"And who am I supposed to shoot?" She glanced up at him. "Of course I plan to shoot you the first opportunity I get. But who else did you have in mind?"

His lips twitched. "I see you haven't lost your spunk. I was beginning to worry." He placed the other gun in his shoulder harness, donned his belt and shoved the knife beneath it. "This is wilderness, Mrs. Stowe, and like you said it will be dark soon. If there are any wild animals nearby, the fire and that gun should make you appear more like a threat and less like dessert."

She felt the color drain out of her face, and her eyes immediately searched the forest. Her pulse skipped. "Animals? What kind of animals do you think might come around?" When she turned her head back in Chance's direction, he was gone.

"Mr. Santana, please. Take a sip. I'm afraid you're getting dehydrated."

The pilot swatted the bottle away. "Leave me alone."

Amanda chewed on her bottom lip and tried again. "You need water, Mr. Santana. Please."

The pilot glared at her. "What difference does it make to you?"

Amanda wondered what she could say to gain his cooperation. She chose to be honest. "I could say that you're a child of God. You're injured, and it's my duty to try and help you survive. Or I could simply say I don't want to be sitting alone out here in the wilderness with a dead body. Which answer do you want to hear?"

Santana half laughed, half sobbed. When he'd regained control, he grinned at her. "You're a feisty little thing, aren't you? That bounty hunter has his hands filled with you. I bet you're going to try and hit him over the head and run off the first chance you get."

"Think so, Mr. Santana? Why? Because it's what you would do?"

He laughed again. "That's right, I would, if my legs weren't pinned under this metal prison." He slammed his fist against the control panel.

"Here." Amanda slipped her left arm under his shoulder blades and supported him while she held the plastic bottle of water to his lips. This time he took a sip. A coughing spasm hit him. When it ceased, exhausted and weak, he placed his head against the side of the plane still intact and closed his eyes. A small dribble of blood flowed from the edge of his mouth down his chin. Amanda knew his injuries were more severe than pinned legs—crushed legs more likely. He probably had internal bleeding, too. And none of it was being helped by the large amounts of alcohol he'd consumed.

"Mr. Santana?"

When he didn't answer, Amanda simply wrapped his blanket tighter and tried to make him as comfortable as she could before slipping outside to wait for the bounty hunter's return.

Chance Walker had been gone for over an hour. Maybe he'd have rescuers with him when he returned. It was not probable but possible. Anything is possible. Maybe someone had seen the wreckage from the air and would be landing with help any minute now. It had been ten hours since the plane crashed. Surely, someone was missing them by now. Someone was initiating a search party.

Amanda crouched beside the dwindling fire. Even

though the air blew the acrid smell of smoke into her lungs, she refused to move back. She threw the last of the wood on the flames and knew the fire wouldn't stay lit much longer. Then, she'd be alone…in the dark. A sense of dread filled her. They were going to die…all three of them…and there was nothing she could do about it.

An inner voice chastised her for her negative thoughts. Surely someone was looking for them. Someone was coming for them. She just needed to have faith.

Another hour had passed, twilight long gone, and Amanda sat in pitch darkness except for the light from the fire. She wrapped her arms around her legs and leaned closer to the welcome heat. She'd gathered all the dead wood she could find, but it was too dark now and much too dangerous to wander more than a few feet from the plane.

Where was Chance? Shouldn't he have been back by now?

She stared into the darkness so hard her eyes burned. What if something had happened to him? What if he wasn't able to come back? What would she do then? She'd be alone in the wilderness without a clue how to survive or how to get back to civilization. Her stomach twisted in knots, and intense fear coursed through her body, clenching her heart, squeezing the breath out of her lungs. A sound caught her attention. Something…or someone… was moving in the brush.

"Chance?"

The rustling sound grew closer. Amanda raised the gun and pointed it in the direction of the noise.

"Chance? Is that you?"

She heard a grunt or a groan—she wasn't sure which. But wouldn't Mr. Walker have called out to her? Her heart skipped a beat when no one answered. She was afraid…so, so afraid. She tried to identify the darker shadow looming toward her. It couldn't be Chance. He stood over six feet tall. This bulky, dark mass was only three or four feet high at best. It must be some kind of animal. But what could it be? It was too short to be a moose, too lumbering to be a mountain cat. She held her breath and watched the dark shadow move closer.

"Who's there?"

Another strange loud grunting reached her ears.

A bear!

Her hands shook as she clasped the gun with both hands and took aim.

Oh my God, help me, be with me in my moment of need.

The lumbering creature broke through the trees.

Amanda fired.

SEVEN

The bullet reached its target, and the animal fell to the ground. A yell of pain pierced the darkness. It took a moment before Amanda could draw a breath, but when she did she panicked. That yell of pain hadn't been an animal's yelp. It was human. Without hesitation, she ran the few yards to the fallen mass lying on the ground. Before she could turn him over, he bolted up to a sitting position and clutched his left arm.

"Are you out of your mind? You shot me." The bounty hunter moved his hand away from his sleeve and stared in astonishment at the blood on his hand.

"I'm sorry. I thought you were a bear."

"A bear?" He muttered unintelligibly under his breath and sprang up.

"That's what you were supposed to do with the weapon. Shoot bears, not me. Besides, didn't I tell you bears are hibernating now?" Standing his full six-four height, he loomed over her, and Amanda found it quite intimidating.

"I…I…"

"Do I look like a bear to you?"

"I called, but you didn't answer."

"I did answer, but I had something in my mouth."

He'd been stooped over, dragging items in a makeshift sling along the ground, carrying objects on his back. That's why in the darkness he had looked so short and wide. He ignored her lame attempts at apologizing, gathered the bulk of objects at his feet and pulled them toward the plane.

She stumbled behind him. "I heard your grunts, but I thought they were bear grunts."

He looked over his shoulder, his swollen, bruised features twisted in disbelief.

"I'm so sorry. Let me help." She reached out for his arm.

"You've helped enough, don't you think?" He hurried toward the fire.

Amanda kept on his heels. "Why didn't you answer me when I called you? You knew I had a gun. You gave it to me, remember? You should have dropped whatever it was you had in your mouth."

They'd reached the fire. Chance dropped the items he'd strung on his back and released his hold on the ones he pulled behind. Shooting her a glare that froze her in place, he held out his hand. "Maybe I should have. Here. This is what I had in my mouth."

She took the Bible from his hands. "I don't know what to say."

"Don't say anything. Just help me get these things sorted and moved into the plane."

He winced, touched his arm lightly and then crouched down beside the fire and began sorting the items he had found scattered in the woods from the crash.

"Thank you."

He nodded, continuing his work without looking up.

"Maybe I should take a look at your arm."

"You just grazed me. I'll be fine. You can help me bandage it later. Right now we need to organize our supplies and get some food in us." He held up his small ax. "I also need to chop some wood or this fire won't last the night."

"You need to take off your coat and your shirt."

Chance glanced up at her. "What?"

"You heard me. You've been shot. I need to tend to the wound."

"I told you it's just a graze. You can tend to it later." He practically growled his words.

"No. We'll tend to it now. I need you strong and in good shape if you're going to help me get back to civilization. I already have one injured man on my hands. I don't need two." She stood as erect as her five-two frame would allow and threw him her sternest look. "If you don't do what I say, then you'll be taking the risk of getting an infection or worse. You'll be of no use to me. Now take off your coat and shirt." When he continued to hesitate, she raised the gun and pointed it straight at him. "Now."

Chance laughed out loud. "I can't believe this. If I don't let you tend to the bullet wound you've already given me, you'll shoot me again? Makes sense to me." Still chuckling, he slipped off his coat and began unbuttoning his shirt.

Amanda leaned inside their shelter and grabbed the first aid kit. When she crawled back out, she looked up and almost choked.

Chance had done as she asked. He stood bare-chested, firelight dancing across the muscles of his chest and arms. For a moment, she couldn't breathe. It wasn't as if she'd never seen a man without a shirt before, she'd been to the beach a thousand times—but she'd never seen Chance Walker without a shirt, and the sight made her heart skip a beat and her pulse race. Then she noted the blood streaming down his left arm and the trembling of his body from the cold.

She placed a hand on his forearm. "Sit down close to the fire. I'll get this bandaged as quickly as I can so you can put your things back on."

Within moments, she determined that he'd been right, and she'd only nicked him. He could use a stitch or two, but that wasn't going to happen. She cleaned the wound with antiseptic, pressed down hard with gauze and then taped it as tightly as possible forming a butterfly stitch, which was better than nothing. The second she finished, Chance shrugged into his shirt and coat and moved so close to the fire she expected him to ignite.

"You're welcome," Amanda said as she put the supplies back into the first aid kit.

"You expect thanks for shooting me and then making me freeze while you bandage the wound you created?" He tipped his cowboy hat. "Okay, thanks." He picked up his ax and headed for the tree limbs he'd dragged in from the woods.

Amanda frowned. What an egotistical, cynical, self-centered...

Her stomach growled loud enough for anyone within a foot or two to hear. She wished she would have listened to the man earlier this morning and forced herself to eat more than a bite or two of her eggs at breakfast. She hadn't had lunch or dinner the day before and nothing to speak of today. Granted she'd never had a large appetite, but right now she could probably eat a man-size steak in record time.

The bounty hunter finished chopping the last of the tree limbs and piled them neatly beside the opening to their shelter. At least there'd be enough wood to get them through the night.

When he threw a couple of logs on the fire, the flames shot up throwing sparks in the air and then settled into a strong, steady burn. The breeze blew a waft of smoke in her face. Amanda coughed and tried to ignore the dryness in her throat.

Her stomach growled again. She knew if she was hungry that Walker had to be starved. Even though he'd eaten a large breakfast, he'd been working nonstop since the crash. He was a big man, and Amanda figured he needed something much more substantial than breakfast to keep his energy up.

Her eyes noted the lines of fatigue on his face as he sat down beside her.

Without saying a word, she reached over and handed him one of the half dozen granola bars she'd taken out of his knapsack.

"Thanks." His black eyes locked with hers. She read the worry in them, saw the exhaustion.

"Did you give some to Santana?" he asked.

She shook her head. "I tried, but I can't seem to get him to stay awake long enough to eat or drink. I'm really worried about him."

Walker grunted. "With good reason."

"How's your arm?" She slowly nibbled on her half of a granola bar. She'd stowed the other half away just in case Santana woke up. Amanda tried to pretend it was a hot meal and a cup of coffee. But her imagination wasn't that good.

He shivered and moved closer to the fire. "I suppose we're both lucky you aren't a better shot."

"I've never fired a gun before." Amanda caught and held his gaze. "And don't say it. I told you I didn't shoot my husband, either."

Chance studied her face in the firelight. "The police found your fingerprints on the gun."

Amanda lowered her eyes. "I picked it up when I saw it lying on the floor."

Chance held up his hand. "Mrs. Stowe, in case you haven't noticed, it has been a horrible day. I'm in no mood to listen to your endless 'I'm innocent' claims."

Amanda recognized the seriousness in his expression so she did as she was told—for now.

Chance watched her in the firelight. She looked tired but alert. Her red eyes told him that she'd been crying, but it must have been while he was gone from camp. In his presence, she seemed determined not to reveal any weakness or vulnerability—and he respected her for that.

The large bump on her forehead caught his attention. It certainly hadn't gone down any. Her eye was still swollen to a mere slit, and now a deep purplish bruise claimed the left side of her face. She'd been hurt in the crash yet never once complained about it. Respect climbed another notch.

While he was gone, Amanda had rummaged through the supplies he'd brought back from the wreckage. She'd found a package of bouillon he'd packed in his duffel bag. He'd brought it along because it took little room and would add taste if he'd been forced to kill a rabbit or squirrel or whatever for his dinner. Although he was grateful he'd been vigilant enough to plan ahead, he couldn't hide his disappointment that he'd been right about needing to take the precautions. This was one time he would have liked to be wrong.

While he was gone, she had heated bottled water by holding it as close to the fire as she could without melting the plastic and then added some of the bouillon. Although it wasn't the best tasting soup in the world, the warm liquid clung to the lining of his stomach and helped ease some of his hunger. He longed to chomp down the remaining two or three granola bars, but he knew they had to ration their food. He didn't look forward to tracking and killing his next meal.

After tonight, they'd also have to start rationing their water. No saying how long it would be before someone found them. He'd already rationed how much he was allowing himself to drink. He just hadn't had the heart to stop her. He glanced over and watched her sip the warm seasoned water. Tonight he'd keep his silence. Tomorrow would be soon enough to drive home the reality of just how dire their situation was.

"You took a nasty hit." He nodded to her forehead. "Does your head hurt?"

She gingerly touched the knot above her eye. "Some. But I can live with it." Then she leaned back against the side of their shelter and looked up into the night sky. "You don't see this kind of thing in the city."

Chance arched an eyebrow and then followed her gaze.

"Stars...millions of them," she said. "You can't see them in the city with all the buildings and streetlights. But here in pitch darkness..." She smiled at him over the fire. "It feels like we're sitting at the gates of heaven."

"Hmm. Apt description. If we're not rescued soon, you might find yourself walking right through those gates of yours."

One look at her horror stricken face and he instantly wished he could pull back his thoughtless words.

Silence stretched between them, becoming more uncomfortable with each passing minute. Grasping for something to talk about—anything to distract her from their perilous situation—he uttered the first words that popped into his head and then regretted them, too.

"Tell me about your husband, Mrs. Stowe."

Amanda blinked a couple of times, staring at him as though she wasn't sure she'd heard him, and then went back to staring at the sky.

"What do you want to know, Mr. Walker?"

Mr. Walker. With everything they'd been through today he'd expected her to call him Chance. Not that it mattered. Anything that maintained a formality between them, built a wall blocking all emotion was a good thing. He didn't want to feel sympathy—or protectiveness—or anything else for that matter toward her. She was nothing more than property—property he had to return in good condition if he wanted to collect his fee.

He watched the glow of firelight dance in her chestnut hair and the warmth of the flames color her cheeks. Her natural beauty drew him to her. Their situation pushed him away.

"How did you meet?" he asked, leaning over and poking the fire with a stick. "At one of those fancy socialite parties?"

"No. We met at a homeless shelter." Before he could scoff, she continued. "I was helping the local mission serve food, and Edward was providing legal services pro bono for a man who had been unjustly accused of burglary."

"Your husband was a lawyer like his father?"

"No again. My husband was nothing like his father. Edward devoted his life to helping those who couldn't help themselves. He worked exclusively with the indigent and those unjustly accused of a crime. The judge, on the other hand, never took a case that didn't further his political career."

"Sounds like you didn't like your father-in-law."

"Not true. Three for three, Mr. Walker. Apparently you don't know me as well as you think you do." She sat up and locked her gaze with his. "I didn't know the judge well enough to like or dislike him. We didn't see Edward's parents often. But they welcomed me into the family and treated me well when we did get together.

"What I didn't like was his parent's heavy disapproval of Edward's career choice. I looked at Edward as a knight-in-shining-armor riding to the defense of the underdog. His parents thought he was wasting his talents. When he passed the bar, they had hoped he'd work for the district attorney's office and build a political career. You know, follow in the judge's footsteps and rub elbows with the rich and powerful.

"His mother, in particular, was very aware of the importance of her son's social standing on a political career, and I think she blamed me for it not being on the scale she wanted. She is quite the socialite, you know. Probably fits the description of one of those women you seem to detest so much."

A tender smile graced her face. "Edward hated the pretence of the social gatherings that posed as charity events. The patrons were more concerned with who wore what and who came with whom than they were with sincerely wanting to help the charity their dollars supported. Edward preferred mingling with ordinary people, hardworking people down on their luck."

"And you? Did you wish Edward would mingle more with the rich and powerful?"

"You think I'm a snob, don't you? But the truth of the matter is that you're the snob." She pierced him with her eyes. "Contempt for people with wealth flows out of every pore of your body. Why is that?"

Chance adjusted his cowboy hat shielding his eyes from her scrutiny. "I dislike anyone who uses their money inappropriately."

"Inappropriately?"

"Yes. The type of people who believe money can buy anything…and anyone. People who refuse to accept the consequences of their own actions and try to buy their way out of trouble." He looked her straight in the eye. "People like you."

She broke eye contact first. "Maybe if you had taken me up on my offer, we wouldn't be trying to survive a frigid night in the wilderness."

A thick, heavy silence stretched between them.

After a moment, Chance stood and glared down at her. He knew his words would be as sharp as knives, but he didn't hold back. "Maybe if *you* hadn't killed that kind, ordinary, knight-in-shining-armor husband of yours and then turned and jumped bail neither one of us would be in this situation. Ever think about that?"

Amanda's eyes blurred with tears. His words had hit their mark. So why did it make him feel like the world's biggest heel?

Chance leaned down and entered the shelter. He checked on a sleeping Santana to make sure he was as warm as possible for the long, frigid night ahead. He rolled out the barrier mat he'd found in the pilot's emergency bag and then spread out the only sleeping bag they had, using it as a cushion between them and the hard, cold floor of the plane.

He glanced over his shoulder every now and then to check on Amanda while he worked. She sat close to the fire, her head bent over that Bible of hers. He didn't know how any one book could be so fascinating, but as long as it kept her calm and cooperative that's all he cared about.

Chance wasn't sure if Santana was asleep or unconscious. But he considered it a blessing either way because the pilot got claustrophobic from being trapped and often broke down into hysterical outbursts. Better he be spared some of the agony being awake caused him.

The tiny space was barely wide enough for the three of them. He'd position Amanda in the middle and make sure she was wrapped tightly in the only remaining blanket. He'd position himself on his side with his back to Amanda and the pilot and face their only opening. This way his body would block the wind from blowing on the two of them. He'd also be the first in line if any curious animal braved the fire and came snooping around.

When he was satisfied with his work, he crawled outside.

Amanda startled when he approached.

"Sorry," he said when he'd seen her jump. "I didn't mean to startle you."

"You didn't. Well, you did, but it wasn't your fault. I was deep in prayer and I just didn't hear you moving around."

"What is that?" Chance asked incredulously and gestured to an evergreen branch sticking up out of the snow. It had a long, silver necklace draped around it like garland.

"It's ten days until Christmas. I saw this branch and thought it made a perfect tiny tree."

"You're decorating Christmas trees? Now?"

"Why not now, Mr. Walker? Christmas is a time of hope. I figured we could use a little of that just about now, don't you?" Amanda patted the silver beads on the necklace. "It's God's promise of new beginnings."

Chance wondered if the puzzlement he felt inside showed in his expression. "You have a strong belief in this God of yours, don't you?"

She nodded and stared at him expectantly.

"Where is God now?" Chance asked. "I'd say you could

use a good dose of his help just about now and I don't see him helping."

A shy smile crossed her lips. "Oh, He's here. He's filling my spirit with peace. He's filling my heart with hope. He's filling my mind with the knowledge that there is nothing…nothing at all that He is going to ask me to go through that He won't be by my side."

Chance lifted his hat and readjusted it on his head as he sat cross-legged by the fire. "How do you know there is a God?"

"How can you look at all of this and believe for one second that there isn't?"

Amanda gestured in a wide sweep of her surroundings and then gasped as she looked up. Luminous green ribbons danced across the sky, and the effect was breathtaking.

"I'd read about this in books, but I've never seen it before."

"The northern lights? I've seen it a dozen or more times. Usually on crisp, cold nights like this one."

They sat in silence and watched the lights sweep across the sky in nature's dance.

"It's one of the most beautiful things I've ever seen," Amanda whispered. "Almost as if God had a paintbrush and was painting the horizon himself."

"Hmm. Back to God again."

"What explanation do you have for all this beauty? The mountains, the stars, the northern lights, the snow, the trees, the complexities of our own bodies? What creator do you honor?"

"Never thought much about it." Chance glanced up at the sky and had to admit the sight felt almost spiritual.

"Maybe you should." Amanda stood up and placed her Bible on the pile of wood by the door. "Good night. Thank you for all you have done to provide a safe and warm place for us for the night." She'd almost disappeared inside the makeshift shelter when she poked her face back out into the firelight.

"God is here for you, too. All you have to do is open your heart and talk to him." She smiled and then disappeared into the darkness.

Chance continued to sit by the fire and stared into the darkness beyond it. He'd heard the term *pitch-black* before but had never experienced it until now. No shadows. No shapes. The outside world ceased to exist, and the only thing left was this fire and the brilliance of the night sky—the gateway to heaven, she'd called it.

He caught a glimpse of the book she'd placed on the edge of the woodpile and picked it up. He ran his hand over the black leather binding. He glanced over his shoulder and could barely make out the two figures inside, but the quiet rhythm of their breathing and the stillness of their bodies told him they were asleep. He turned his attention back to the item in his hand.

What made this book so special? How had it been able to calm her in one of the most stressful, life-threatening moments of her life? What secrets were inside these covers?

He glanced over his shoulder again. When he assured himself that both Amanda and Santana were asleep, he opened the Bible and began to read.

EIGHT

Jeff "Lucky" Lupine's stomach growled when the aroma of grilled meat and freshly brewed coffee greeted him. The sound of his boots clunking against the wooden floor as he moved across the room went unnoticed amid the low rumble of conversations from neighboring tables as he made his way to the back.

He'd been coming to Rhoda's broken-down shack regularly for the past few months, recognized most of the faces, bothered with none. Lucky had learned long ago that the people who chose to make their home in this desolate part of Alaska were usually on the run from something—the law, ex-wives, themselves. He grinned to himself, realizing he fit all three categories.

Lucky chose a spot near the rear exit where he could sit with his back against the wall. It provided him with a good view of the room as well as everyone entering or exiting the building. In his line of work, it paid to be aware of his surroundings, though he'd never had to worry about Rhoda's regulars poking their noses into his business. He wished he could say the same about Rhoda.

He'd barely plopped his butt in a chair when she appeared at his side.

"You're running a little late today aren't you, Lucky?"

The woman squeezed her ample girth into the space beside him. "I was thinking maybe you were away on a job or something." She set a coffee cup in front of him with her left hand. "I've been listening to the weather reports. They've been forecasting near-blizzard conditions headed this way. It sure wouldn't be a good time for you to be making deliveries with that plane of yours." She filled the cup from the pot in her right hand. "Unusual for this early in the season. Must be global warming."

Global warming. Rhoda's favorite political platform.

Lucky rolled his eyes and swallowed his annoyance. If she didn't serve the best tasting food this side of Fairbanks at a dirt cheap price, he'd probably make her wish she'd kept her nose in her own business. But instead of venting his irritation, he simply shrugged.

"Had a late night last night. Guess I slept in."

"So I should probably keep the coffee comin, huh?"

The thought of her continually returning to his table soured his stomach. He slapped the table in front of him. "I got a better idea. Why don't you just leave that pot?"

Rhoda shrugged but did as requested. "Usual order?"

Lucky nodded and she hurried away.

He was on his second cup of coffee when she returned with breakfast, and he dove into it with relish. He'd been keeping a close watch on the weather, too. He knew the impending winter storm would throw a wrench in his search for the missing plane. His only consolation was if he didn't find the missing plane today that the storm would finish them off for sure.

Satisfied that he'd stoked up for the long day ahead, he pushed his plate to the side and spread out the map. Lucky marked off the territory he'd already covered and compared it to the route he'd planned to take today. He checked and double-checked his coordinates, grinned and took a swig of his coffee. He'd find them today. He was certain of it. And then he'd be able to get his boss off his back.

Although he hadn't heard a word since their phone conversation yesterday, just the thought of having to report that he couldn't find the bodies caused him to break out in a cold sweat. He was no fool. He knew all too well what his boss did about loose ends, and he wasn't intending to be one of them.

Chance dropped the wood he collected earlier this morning next to the pile left over from last night. Voices drifted out from inside the shelter. He paused a moment, listened and then realized that Amanda was saying a prayer. What stopped Chance in his tracks was the sound of Santana's voice joining her.

Unable to believe his ears, he crouched down and looked inside. Amanda, leaning with her back against the control panel, faced the entrance, her Bible resting on her lap. She glanced up when she heard him enter.

"Good morning."

"Morning." He moved inside and sat down so he wouldn't accidentally pull down the tarp. "Good to see you're awake, Mr. Santana. How are you feeling?"

"I'm still trapped in this metal coffin. How do you think I feel?" Santana grumbled. He nodded at the Bible in Amanda's lap. "I figure that book helped her on the flight, maybe a prayer or two would do me some good just about now." He gasped and started to cough. "The way my luck's been running, I probably won't make it through today anyway."

"Don't say that, Mr. Santana," Amanda said and patted a dry cloth against his lips. "Don't give up hope. I'm sure we're going to be rescued today."

Santana laughed humorlessly, and then his body was racked with coughing again.

"In case anyone does fly over," Chance said, "one of us should be outside by the fire at all times." Chance caught and held Amanda's gaze. "I want to instruct you on how to use the flares just in case you see a plane fly over when I'm not around."

Amanda frowned. "Why wouldn't you be around?"

Chance adjusted his Stetson, stalling for time while he considered how to reply so he wouldn't upset the two of them. How do you tell someone that not only do you not believe help will find you in time but that if he didn't find some food—and soon—they would starve to death? He decided under the circumstances that fabricating a reason wouldn't do anyone any good so he opted for the truth.

"This time of year there's only about five or six hours of daylight. I'm going to need the light for hunting."

Amanda frowned. "The granola bars are gone, but don't we still have some packages of dried fruit?"

Chance nodded. "Yes, but I don't think a small bag of dried fruit is going to be enough to keep our energy level up. We're burning more calories than we're taking in. Besides, there's no guarantee I'm going to catch anything. This time tomorrow we're going to want something more substantial than dried fruit."

"Tomorrow?" Amanda paled. "I thought you expected a rescue plane to be flying over today. Isn't that why you're showing me how to set off the flares?"

"Yes. But just in case…"

Amanda shook her head as if she couldn't believe what she'd heard. "Of course, just in case." Her tone of voice was laced with sarcasm. "I almost forgot. You have to plan for every possibility, don't you? You have this need to always be right."

Anger sent a wave of warmth up his neck. "When your stomach is cramping with hunger pangs, I think you're going to be happy I am the way I am."

"I don't plan to find out. I'm expecting us to be rescued later today."

"Ahh, yes. How could I forget? The eternal optimist. Little Miss Sunshine who believes an invisible God will magically see her through every storm."

Amanda caught her breath but held his gaze. "It's called faith. You ought to try it."

Chance broke eye contact and went back outside. The woman infuriated him. It was like she knew every one of his hot buttons and calmly and repeatedly hit every one. But he had to admit that anger wasn't the only emotion she evoked in him. His mind conjured up a picture of how she looked lost in sleep last night—small, vulnerable and *innocent*.

Those thoughts made him even more uncomfortable. When she looked at him with those big, brown eyes—or planted her hands on her hips and prepared for battle—or rivaled the sun when she smiled up at him, his heart melted. He hated to admit it, but she brought out the "macho man" in him. He wanted to impress her. He wanted to protect her. He wanted to *release* her. And he hated himself for that weakness.

Deciding to work off some of his pent-up tension, he shook off his coat for more ease of motion and began chopping the wood he'd gathered. His movements settled into a steady rhythm. He almost laughed out loud when after a few minutes he realized the absurdity of his thoughts. Unconsciously he'd been humming a childhood chant as he kept time with each swing. *She likes me. She likes me not.*

NINE

After a few moments, Amanda followed Chance out of the shelter and stood quietly at the entrance. He seemed larger than life against the Alaskan backdrop, filling her senses, stealing her breath. He was a tall man—strong, intimidating. Yet she felt safe and protected in his presence.

The blustery bravado gone, he seemed intent on the task at hand. She could see the muscles in his arms strain against his flannel shirt as he hoisted the ax and swung it over and over again.

Sensing her presence, he paused. His dark eyes fixed on her and the whole world stopped. There were no sounds, no rustling from the woods, no twittering of birds, not even the sound of their breathing filled the air. They simply stared at each other. Their gazes communicated thoughts and feelings neither one of them were brave enough to speak aloud.

"What do you want?" he asked.

The deep, resonating sound of his voice slithered along her spine. What did she want? Every breath in her body screamed *you*. Confusion and fear made her break eye contact. She picked up one of the flares lying on the ground.

"You wanted to show me how to use this."

The knowing look in his eyes told her he hadn't missed

the breathiness in her voice or the sudden heat in her cheeks.

He stepped closer.

Too close.

His hand wrapped around the flare she held in hers. The unexpected warmth of his skin against her fingertips caused a knot to form in her stomach and her pulses raced.

Black hair jutted out from beneath his cowboy hat, and she wondered what it would feel like to run her fingers through it. Did he ever take that hat off? The thought made her smile.

His body blocked the sun. The musky scent of male mixed with pine teased her senses. She tried to guess his age and placed him about ten years older than either Edward or herself, probably in his mid-thirties. His tanned skin at this time of year told her he spent considerable time outdoors.

She continued staring at him, her gaze tracing the small, crinkled lines at the edges of the most dark, piercing eyes she had ever seen. And his lips...she couldn't move her eyes away from those inviting male lips. What would they feel like pressed against her own?

"What do you really want from me?" His low, rumbling voice breathed across her face in a hot whisper.

Her legs wobbled beneath her, and her hands trembled. What was happening to her? How could she possibly be attracted to this man? She was a widow and still grieving. She missed Edward every single day of her life. He'd been her best friend. Yet this stranger pulled at her senses, played with her mind and stirred her emotions. And he wasn't just any stranger. This man was a threat in more ways than one. He intended to rob her of her freedom.

"Tell me." Chance wrapped his arm around her waist and pulled her against him. "Tell me what you want."

The tension between them was thick and heavy.

Amanda's heart beat wildly, and she thought it might grow wings and fly right out of her chest. She wet her lower lip with her tongue and stared up at him. "I want my freedom, Chance."

Her words struck him with a force so strong a person might think she had physically hit him. Instantly he released his hold on her waist and put a considerable distance between them.

"And I hope with the help of a good attorney that that will happen for you." He donned his coat, lifted his hat and ran a fast sweep through his hair before settling it back on his head.

"Be cautious. We only have two flares. If you hear a plane while I'm gone, wait until you actually see it before you release the flare. Then watch closely. They'll turn around or tip their wings to let you know they've seen you." He sheathed his knife on his waistband and then buttoned his coat. "I'll be back before dark."

Then he was gone.

Amanda tried to keep a positive attitude, but it was becoming more difficult as the day progressed. She couldn't believe that it had only been twenty-four hours since their plane crashed. In many ways, it felt like weeks.

Daylight hours were quickly fading. She'd stayed by the fire most of the day, only going in occasionally to check on Mr. Santana. But she hadn't seen or heard anything. No planes. No hunters. Just the roar of silence.

Amanda worried about the pilot. If help didn't come soon… She allowed her thoughts to drift away. She knew deep inside that there wasn't going to be any help for Santana. The best she could do was to keep him as warm and comfortable as possible, help him with his prayers and not let him die alone.

Her eyes searched the skies. Nothing. Not even a bird passed by. Shouldn't there be a search party by now? She hadn't expected anyone yesterday. By the time the control tower had realized they'd crashed and put the gears in motion to launch a rescue they would have been fighting against time.

Daylight and Alaskan winters didn't mix.

But today...today she had truly believed there would be a plane. She was having difficulty keeping her tears at bay as she dealt with the deep disappointment that there hadn't been one.

The reality of the current situation pressed on her heart like a heavy weight, and she was finding it harder to hold on to the hope that things would begin to turn around for her. Losing Edward had broken her heart. Being charged with his murder stunned her. Then that mysterious call— from a *mistress.* How could Edward have done that to her? To them?

Amanda thought she had cried all the tears she was capable of shedding, but when she wiped the wetness from her cheeks she began to think this pain would never go away, these tears would never end.

Oh, Edward, what happened to us? How did something so beautiful and precious turn into something so ugly?

Not so long ago they were holding hands and planning children. Now she was fighting to survive, stranded in the wilderness with a bounty hunter and a dying pilot. And for the first time she was starting to believe it was possible they weren't going to get out of here.

Amanda had prayed for rescue, for a way out of the whole murder mess she was in. Although she knew God was with her and nothing could shake her faith, she was beginning to believe that maybe God's answer to her prayers might be "no."

Her stomach growled with hunger. She hadn't had a full meal for two days and she found herself getting light-headed, even a little nauseous. She hated to face Chance's "I-told-you-so" attitude, but he was right. They needed food. And sooner rather than later would be good.

Her eyes searched the woods. There was no sign of Chance. He'd been gone all day. She hated to admit it, but she was so hungry she didn't care what he dragged back. She'd find a way to cook it.

Angry with herself that she was still crying, she wiped the moisture off her cheeks when she realized it wasn't tears but was snow! Big, wet snowflakes melted on her eyelashes and dusted her hair and clothing. Within minutes, the dusting intensified, and snow fell like white rain. The wind picked up and the snow quickly covered not only everything in sight on the ground but it limited visibility to no more than a dozen feet.

Hoping the force of the storm wouldn't extinguish the flames, Amanda threw two more logs on the fire. She cupped her hand over her eyes and scanned the woods. Why hadn't Chance returned? Would he be able to find his way back in this weather?

Amanda shivered, and her teeth chattered. The cold penetrated every cell, muscle and bone in her body, the frigid air piercing to inhale. She couldn't stay outside any longer. Her clothes were getting wet, and her hands were turning numb. She turned to go inside the shelter when she heard it. The sound stopped her in her tracks and she listened intently.

Yes! She wasn't imagining it. She had heard the engine

of an approaching plane. Excited and giddy, she laughed out loud, grabbed the flare and searched the skies. She'd see it any minute now. Help was on the way!

TEN

Lucky didn't feel very lucky right about now. The heavy gray clouds that had threatened ill weather for hours finally fulfilled their promise and were emptying on the Alaskan landscape.

He slammed the U-shaped steering wheel with the palm of his hand. He didn't want to give up. It wasn't doing his disposition any good to have to return home without answers for a second day in a row. But he wasn't stupid. No one in their right mind flew in an Alaskan blizzard—not if they intended to land in one piece that is.

Lucky banked the plane to the right and was coming into a full turn when he caught a glint of light out of the corner of his eye. Was that the sun reflecting off metal? He couldn't risk not checking it out.

He brought the plane full circle and strained his eyes looking for the downed plane—evergreens and snow, more evergreens, more snow. He couldn't see a thing through this lousy storm. He muttered a string of expletives and was just about to set his course for home when a flare lit the horizon.

He whooped and hollered. He'd found them. He knew he would.

The heavy snowfall and blustery winds made visibility nearly impossible. He wouldn't be able to do anything about them today. He had to get home while he was still able.

But he wasn't worried. He knew where to find them now. Even if they had managed to survive the crash, no way would they be able to survive the night. They had to have minimal supplies, minimal shelter and the first major storm of the winter was dumping right on top of them.

No, they wouldn't make it through the night. Lucky grinned so wide his face hurt. And if by some crazy twist of fate they did survive, he hoped they enjoyed their last night on Earth. Because, without a doubt, tomorrow they were going to die.

Chance threw a couple more logs on the fire, stomped as much snow as possible off his boots and crept inside the shelter.

"What were you thinking?" he asked, barely able to conceal the weariness in his voice.

Amanda took one look at him and quipped, "And they say the abominable snowman is just a myth."

He brushed more snow from the sleeve of his coat. "I'm not kidding. I told you not to fire one of those flares unless you saw a plane."

He flopped down beside her, his back toward the fire, ice crystals melting from his eyelashes and the rim of his hat. "And up here the monster is known as a yeti."

Amanda was so happy he had made it back in one piece all she could do was grin. She brushed some of the snow off his other sleeve and said, "I told you already. I did see a plane."

"I didn't see or hear anything."

Amanda laughed up at him, staring into his dark eyes circled with fatigue. "Maybe you're blind and deaf. How do I know? I'm telling you I saw a plane flying really low. I fired the flare just minutes before he flew right over me."

"Did he circle around?"

"No."

"Tip his wings?"

"Not that I noticed. But he had to see me. I waited until he got really close before I fired the flare."

"What kind of plane was it?" Chance shifted his weight, withdrew his gun from his shoulder harness and placed it within hand's reach.

"It was a tiny one like this except it had cigar-shaped wheels."

"Cigar-shaped wheels? Are you trying to say it was a seaplane?"

"I'm trying to tell you that I don't know what kind of plane it was and I don't care. As far as I'm concerned right now it's a rescue plane. It saw us. I know it did. And even if it missed me waving my arms, I know it saw my flare. When it's daylight it will come back and bring help. You'll see."

Chance reached over and ever so gently brushed a strand of her hair out of her face.

Amanda's breath caught in her throat at the sudden intimate gesture. They stared into each other's eyes. Amanda was the first to speak.

"You must be exhausted. You were gone all day. Did you have any luck?"

He flopped onto his back and covered his eyes with the back of his hand. "I not only didn't catch anything, but I didn't even *see* anything. Nothing. Not a bird. A squirrel. I would have even settled for a field mouse. If I didn't know better, I'd say we're the only living creatures on Earth right about now."

Amanda giggled, and the sound filled the air like wind

chimes in a gentle summer breeze. She crawled to the end of the sleeping bag and then back again.

"Here," she said. "I saved you a few pieces of dried fruit. Mr. Santana and I already ate our share."

He waved it away. "No. Save it for tomorrow."

Amanda shoved it back at him. "Stop trying to be such a macho man and eat."

His stomach growled as if on cue.

"See. At least part of your body is working even if your brains aren't. Now eat."

She was hungry. She'd never been so hungry before in her life, but she knew he needed the nourishment more than she did. She was depending on him to keep them alive. Besides, it was water her body craved the most. They'd finished the last of the bottled water late last night, and her mouth was so dry it felt stuffed with cotton balls. She'd considered sucking on snow, but she'd read somewhere that it took excessive body energy to do that. She didn't know if it was true or not, but she knew her energy was as depleted as she could afford right about now.

"Do what she says," Santana said in a hoarse whisper. "Twenty-four hours with the lady and even I know once she sets her mind to something there's no talking her out of it."

Amanda laughed and pushed the bag into Chance's hand.

He pulled a piece of fruit out of the bag, popped it in his mouth and just let it sit there as he savored the taste of it.

"Besides," Amanda said, unable to contain her excitement from spilling over into her voice, "they know where we are now. They'll be back in the morning to rescue us."

"No one's coming to rescue us," Santana said. "If they didn't tip their wings or turn around, then they didn't see you so they won't be coming back." A cough racked his body from the effort it took to speak.

The atmosphere in the shelter became tense. Chance perched himself up on one elbow and stared at the pilot, staying ominously quiet.

Amanda sat up between the two of them. She patted Santana on the forearm. "Of course he'll be back. You'll see. Why don't you try and get some sleep?"

"Nobody's coming," the man yelled.

Amanda tried to comfort him. "It will be okay, Mr. Santana. Even if this plane didn't see us, the next one will. Don't you see? They're looking for us now, so it's only a matter of time."

Santana shook his head, and tears streamed down his face.

Amanda was shocked and didn't quite know how to respond.

"What aren't you telling us?" The low, steely tone in Chance's voice seemed to make the man shrivel into himself.

Chance sat up. "What are you not telling us, Santana?"

"Chance, leave him alone." Amanda put her other hand on Chance's arm and suddenly felt like she was sitting between two pit bulls getting ready to shed blood. "He's delirious. He doesn't know what he's saying."

"I'm sorry," Santana whimpered. "I'm so sorry."

Chance lunged forward with lightning speed, edging her out of the way and grabbing the pilot by the front of his coat.

"What are you sorry about, Santana?"

"Chance, stop it. Leave him alone." Amanda pulled on his arm, but it had no effect.

"I needed the money. And they were paying me more

than I'd seen in months." The pilot lowered his head and sobbed.

"You better talk to me." Chance shook the man. "Right now!"

Amanda sat back on her feet and watched the scene unfold like it was a bad dream.

"Nobody's coming to rescue us because nobody knows we're here." Santana coughed and then coughed again. "I filed a fake flight plan. Even if someone did decide to look for us, they'd be looking hundreds of miles in the wrong direction."

An ominous, deadly silence fell upon the shelter.

Amanda stared at the pilot in shock.

Suddenly, Chance started shaking him violently. "Why didn't you tell us sooner? Why?"

"Chance!" Amanda sprang into action, jumping on the bounty hunter's back and trying to pull him off of the pilot. "Chance, stop! You're hurting him!"

Almost as though coming out of a deep fog, Chance froze and then slowly released his hold on the man's coat.

Amanda moved away but never took her eyes off of him.

He took several long, deep breaths, obviously trying to get his emotions back under control.

The only sound in the shelter was Santana's sobs.

"Who paid you to file a false flight plan?" Walker asked.

"I don't know." Santana lifted his hands up to protect his face when he saw Chance loom over him. "I swear."

Chance stared at the man but remained under control. "How did you get the money?"

"Through the friend of a friend. They dropped off a package of bills for me at Rhoda's bar. I never knew who the money came from."

"Where were you supposed to take us?"

"An old landing field about three hundred miles south of here. I was supposed to drop you off and leave. End of story."

"End of story?"

The suppressed rage in Chance's tone of voice frightened Amanda. She'd never seen this side of him, and she had no idea what he might be capable of.

"No. Not end of story." Walker spat the words out through tightly clenched teeth. "Why did they want us dropped off in an abandoned field? What were their plans?"

"I don't know. I swear."

"You didn't ask? You just accepted a package of money and never asked any questions? Is that what you're telling me?"

The pilot nodded. "Up here, it's best to mind your own business. As far as I was concerned, the deal was to fly you to the field, drop you off and go home. That's all I knew, and that's all I wanted to know."

He lowered his arms and looked directly into Chance's face. "I'm sorry. I really am."

Chance sat back. His shoulders sagged, and the breath seemed to seep out of him. He looked like a fighter who had just lost the last match.

"Why?" His voice sounded weary, defeated. "Why didn't you tell us all of this yesterday?"

Santana dropped his eyes. "I was afraid if you knew that you would try and walk out of here. You'd leave me behind, and I didn't want to die alone." Santana's sobs filled the tiny shelter.

Amanda was so shocked she couldn't speak. She stared at Chance and hoped she had just imagined the entire scene. Water deprivation—that was it. She was hallucinating and didn't even know it.

Without speaking another word, Chance crawled out of the shelter and disappeared from sight.

Amanda bit her lip in frustration. She hated the way he kept disappearing and leaving her behind to fend for herself. Well, this time she wasn't going to let him get away with it. She jumped to her feet and hurried after him.

ELEVEN

Chance stood on the other side of the fire, threw his hands in the air and bellowed long and loud in frustration. They had been sitting in frigid temperatures without food or water for going on two days. Two days! They were waiting for help that wasn't going to come.

Because he was afraid, Santana had been more than willing to sentence them to a torturous death in this frigid wasteland.

So die with company? Would that really make him feel better?

He tried to put himself in Santana's position, trapped, knowing his own greed assured no rescue and terrified the other occupants of the plane would leave him defenseless against the elements and possible predators. Maybe Chance might have been more empathetic if the fool hadn't involved Amanda.

A fresh wave of rage washed over him.

He might have been able to save her life if they'd left yesterday right after the crash. They wouldn't be suffering like they were now from exhaustion, dehydration and hunger. They might have made it to a creek. There are a multitude of waterways in Alaska. Or maybe he would have stumbled upon a homestead or a hunter's cabin. But now—

The image of Amanda's trusting brown eyes flashed through his mind. He knew she believed he would be able to keep them alive until help arrived. How was she going to look at him now that help wasn't coming? What would he see when she realized he wasn't able to just walk her out of danger and into safety?

Chance had to lower his eyes against the force of the falling snow. For the first time since this nightmare had begun, he began to wonder if falling asleep and dying from hypothermia might not be a blessing for all of them. At least he wouldn't have to watch Amanda starve to death or hallucinate from dehydration or freeze to death when the last match for a fire was gone. He didn't think he could bear to see despair or fear in her eyes—or worse, disappointment in him.

Now who was being selfish?

He shook the snow off his hat, put it back on and once again looked up at the sky.

If Amanda's right and you really are up there, God, we sure could use some helpful intervention right about now.

His eyes searched the heavens. She'd sworn there'd been a low-flying plane. Amanda understood the necessity of holding on to the flares. She would never have wasted one foolishly.

But why hadn't the pilot of that plane acknowledged the flare? Why didn't he circle back around or tip his wings or indicate in any way that he'd seen her and would send help?

Those unanswered questions created a dark, creeping fear to lodge in the pit of his stomach and filled him with an ominous foreboding.

Someone had gone to a lot of trouble to make sure

Amanda was not returned to police custody. Maybe the case against her wasn't as strong as he originally assumed. Maybe the real killer couldn't afford to have the police start considering other suspects.

Would that same someone be desperate enough to sabotage a plane? Would they fly over to make sure the plane had crashed? And when they realized Amanda had survived the crash, would they be coming back to finish the job?

Well, the time for sitting in this death trap and doing nothing to save themselves was over. He knew he'd be faced with major opposition. Amanda wouldn't want to leave Santana alone but, whether she liked it or not, tomorrow they were going to walk out of here.

"Chance?"

He spun around at the sound of Amanda's voice. She looked so beautiful in the firelight. Golden highlights danced in her hair. The warmth of the fire toasted her cheeks with a rosy hue. He wanted to pull her close, hold her near, protect her from harm. Too late now. He gave a self-deprecating laugh. Who was going to protect her from him—and all his mistakes and misjudgments?

"What are you doing out here?" he asked.

"Looking for you." Her voice slid like a gentle caress along his nerve endings. She'd trusted him and he'd failed her. He'd promised himself he would protect her no matter what—or die trying.

Well, at least he'd be able to keep half of that promise.

Amanda stepped closer. Snow draped her hair like a white mantle. Flakes clung to her eyelashes. The cold tinged her nose and cheeks a bright red.

"I…I was worried," she said, a husky note in her voice. "You were so upset when you left. And then I heard you yell…" She caught his gaze and held it. "Are you okay?"

He moved toward her, brushing the snow from her hair, touching her cheek with his hand.

He didn't see her as Amanda Stowe, prisoner, anymore. When he looked into her eyes, all he saw was kindness, trust and hope.

Unable to resist, he pulled her into his arms and kissed her. It wasn't a tender kiss. It was a passionate, demanding, almost desperate one. He should have at least heard her out, given her the chance to tell her side of the story.

Now…

Chance wanted to believe in her. And he desperately wanted her to know it. He told her with his eyes. He told her with his kiss. He hoped his actions revealed more in those few seconds than his words ever could.

And in that moment, with snow swirling above them, around them, on them—enveloping them in the dark stillness of this wilderness—Amanda did not resist.

For one crazy, spontaneous moment she returned his kiss, matching his passion, exposing her vulnerability to him, her trust, her belief in his innate goodness. She seemed to melt into the shelter of his arms. She burrowed against his strength.

And then the moment passed.

Sanity, caution, remorse shoved their way to the surface and buried those warm, wonderful feelings Amanda had brought out in him. His mind flashed back to another woman, another love, another betrayal. Instantly, he released her and stepped away.

She stared at him in the firelight, those big brown eyes of hers looking confused, bewildered.

"That shouldn't have happened." He lowered his gaze. "I'm sorry. It won't happen again."

She held her fingers to her lips but remained silent,

watching him, almost as if she expected him to say something more but for the life of him he didn't know what.

"You better get some sleep," Chance said. "We're leaving first thing in the morning."

She blinked. "But we can't leave Mr. Santana." A look of panic flashed across her face. "He can't tend the fire. He can't even protect himself if a wolf or some other wild animal comes into camp. We can't leave. He'll die without our help."

"*We'll* die if we don't." He locked his gaze with hers and then washed a hand over his bearded stubble. "Look, the reality of the situation is that he's going to die anyway. We need to try and save ourselves."

A look of horror flashed across her face when she realized he was serious and they were going to leave the man trapped and alone.

"I can't…" She took a step back. "I won't."

Chance grabbed her forearm. "Don't you understand? You heard him. He filed a fake flight plan. No one is looking for us. We're on our own."

"But there was a plane…"

"Amanda, listen to me." He tightened his grip on her arm. "Did you ever stop to think that maybe we crashed for a reason? That maybe the fake flight plan and the crash were part of a scheme to keep you from returning."

A look of shock and horror filled her eyes. "No. That's not true." She tried to pull free, but he held her fast.

"Amanda, trust me." He locked his gaze with hers. "We only have ourselves to rely on now. We have to try to make it out of here or we're going to die. And I don't know about you but I'd rather die fighting to live than sit here waiting to die." He let go of her arm. "Besides, we're the only chance Santana has. He needs us to bring equipment back to free him. The longer we wait, the more likely he is to die."

He could see her wrestling with her emotions. She knew he was right. He could see it in her eyes. And she knew the chances for their own survival would lessen with each passing day. But the idea of walking away while the pilot was trapped, helpless and alone...her compassion wouldn't let her come to grips with it.

"I can't." Tears filled her eyes. "It's so cruel."

He knew he had to take the responsibility away from her if he expected her to be able to go.

"You act like I'm giving you a choice." He glared at her with as much intimidation as he could muster. "This time tomorrow you will be walking out of here with me— in handcuffs if you insist. Now get some sleep because I don't want to have to carry you out of here. But make no mistake. If I have to, I will."

He watched Amanda turn slowly and go back inside the shelter. He tried to erase from his mind the contempt he saw on her face. He was trying to save her life, but he wondered if she'd ever forgive him for it.

Amanda stretched her arms above her head and twisted her body like a lazy cat as she pulled herself out of sleep. Frigid air blew across her body and shocked her into awareness. Her eyes flew open, and she found herself staring out at the woods and not at the solid wall of Chance's back she'd awoken to yesterday.

She leaned up on one elbow and glanced around. Where was Chance?

She sat up and wiped the sleep from her eyes.

The snow had stopped—unfortunately, not before it had extinguished their fire. Her teeth chattered from the cold. She hugged her arms tightly around her torso trying to control the shivers that racked her body.

Turning to check that Santana's blankets were tucked tightly around him, Amanda froze. She didn't need to touch his still, rigid body to know he had died during the night. After what he had done, she was surprised she felt a tear roll down her cheek. But even though he had done a despicable thing, he was still a human being who had died a terrible, tragic death.

She bowed her head and prayed.

When she finished, she gently pulled his blanket over his face and moved out of the shelter. The first thing she noted was two overstuffed packs sitting by the extinguished fire ring. It looked like Chance had shoved everything they could possibly hope to carry with them into his duffel bag and into the pilot's small emergency bag. He'd even opened up one of his flannel shirts, stuffed it with items and used the arms as a tie that could be laced and carried on a branch.

Yep. Chance wasn't kidding. They were leaving today. And now that the pilot was dead, Amanda had to admit there was no reason to stay. She was ready to go home… no matter what future waited for her there.

She shielded her eyes against the sunlight as she searched the horizon for some sign of Chance. She saw his footprints in the newly fallen snow leading into the woods and decided to follow. After all, there was nothing holding her here anymore.

She'd barely gone more than a couple of dozen yards into the woods when a second set of prints then a third and a fourth caught and held her attention. She stooped down for a closer look. Wolves! The tracks had been coming from a different direction, blended with Chance's footprints here and then both wolf and human tracks headed to the rise.

Oh God, help us.

Amanda raced back to the plane wreckage. She knew she was wasting precious time, but warning Chance wouldn't be enough. She needed a weapon. She dug frantically through the luggage. As the seconds ticked by, she began to panic. Where was it? She glanced up in frustration and then she saw it—resting on top of the woodpile. She should have known that Chance would never have left her unprotected.

She grabbed the weapon and raced into the woods, following the tracks uphill as quickly as her legs would carry her. She cleared the woods, reached the top of the rise and panicked. Her breath locked in her throat, and her legs shook this time from fear not cold.

Facing away from her less than a dozen yards ahead, five gray wolves paced sniffing the air and moving closer with each arc toward Chance.

Chance stood to her right, facing in her direction and not moving. He had his gun drawn and pointed in the wolves direction, but because it was impossible to hit all of them, he hadn't yet pulled the trigger.

Her presence seemed to upset the wolves. Their body language became more frenzied with each passing moment.

One of the wolves stopped, faced Chance and howled. It crept forward a dozen steps and howled again.

The sound was not like anything Amanda had ever heard before. Every hair on her body rose in fear. Her heart pounded so hard it was almost painful to breathe as she forced herself to inhale. Slowly, she raised her weapon and prayed she wouldn't have to use it. The small-caliber pistol seemed like she would be trying to stop a train with a squirt gun.

Noise! She had read that loud, sudden noises frightened wolves and they'd run away. Maybe she should scream, yell, fire her weapon in the air.

Before she could decide what to do, she heard it.

An engine. The plane from yesterday was coming back.

She stared at the horizon wishing the plane into existence, praying it there—and then it was. Flying so low it could almost touch the ground, the fast-moving airplane grew closer by the second.

She began to scream, jump up and down and wave her arms. Amanda didn't know whether it was her screaming or the sound of the fast approaching plane that frightened the animals but within seconds the pack of wolves raced off in the opposite direction.

Amanda screamed with glee. "See, Chance? There had been a plane yesterday." She jumped and danced her way into the clearing. It hadn't been her imagination, and now the plane had returned to rescue them.

A puzzled expression crossed her face as she watched the plane approach. She couldn't believe her eyes. Instead of slowing down to land, it seemed to be gaining speed. It was not only speeding up—it seemed intent on running Chance down!

She watched in horror as he turned and ran, the plane's propellers closing the distance between them with amazing speed. The plane was almost on top of him when Amanda heard him yell and dive over the side.

The plane kept going, rising every second she watched it.

Amanda raced toward the cliff. Terrified at what she might see, she whispered a prayer for strength and tried to force herself to look over the edge. She threw herself on the ground, crawled to the side and tried to look over the edge.

Her fear of heights paralyzed her and twisted her stomach into painful knots. Black dots danced in front of her eyes, and she felt like she might pass out.

Control yourself! You have to look over the side. A second wave of terror paralyzed her, and tears of frustration slid down her face.

You can do this. You have to do this. Chance needs you.

She dropped to the ground, dug her hands beneath the snow, clinging to whatever solid surface she could find, and inched closer to the edge. She swallowed a breath and moved another inch.

Do this for Chance. He needs you. Move.

Grateful for the voice in her head, Amanda locked all other thoughts out of her mind and slowly, but with determination, she crawled forward another inch until she was on the edge of the precipice and forced herself to look down.

Chance lay sprawled across a boulder jutting out of the mountainside. He lay still, unmoving.

"Chance!" She could barely control her emotions when he didn't respond. He couldn't be dead. He couldn't. She rose to a sitting position, cupped her hands, leaned forward and screamed his name again. There was still no response.

She had to climb down to him.

The thought made her nauseous, and for the first time in days, she was grateful her stomach was empty. She searched for a way down and couldn't find one. There was nothing to hold on to—no path to follow. She didn't have a rope to tie around her waist to lower herself. How was she going to reach him?

"Chance!" Her body heaved with sobs at the hopelessness of the situation.

Maybe she could jump. That rock wasn't that far down. It was a pretty large outcropping and seemed to have plenty of room for two of them. But what would happen if she did jump? How would she get both of them back up to the top of the rise? What if she jumped and missed? Worse, what if she did jump, got trapped on the boulder and Chance was already dead?

All these thoughts swirled through her mind and sent waves of panic from her head to her toes. But then she realized that none of it mattered. She had to get down there to see if she could help Chance. If he was already dead or if she misjudged the jump were things she couldn't control and wouldn't know until she tried. She sat for a moment contemplating the safest way to do what she knew she had to do and then put their lives in God's hands.

When she was sure of her strategy—or as sure as she could be under the circumstances—she stood up and moved to the edge of the cliff. If she stayed close to the side of the mountain and just stepped into space, she should make it. The outcropping was about twenty feet below where she stood now. She could do this. She *would* do this—for Chance.

She closed her eyes and lifted her foot.

It was the sound of the plane returning that made her freeze in space and open her eyes. It had circled around and was coming back low, fast and heading right for her.

Amanda turned and ran. She ran faster than she believed she could and headed toward the cover of the evergreens. She had almost reached the woods when she heard loud popping noises. What was that?

The ground around her kicked up in a dozen different places, and holes appeared in the snow. Someone was shooting at her! She didn't think she could but adrenaline kicked in and she moved faster—a dozen yards to safety, five yards, five feet.

Suddenly, it felt like someone had punched her in the back with a force that knocked her off her feet. She refused to stop. She scrambled through the snow, clearing the last few feet and hiding in the evergreens knowing the plane couldn't follow, couldn't see her.

She leaned back against a tree trunk and tried to catch her breath. She could hear the sound of the plane's engine fading. He was gone—at least, for now. Why was someone trying to kill her? *Who* was trying to kill her? A searing heat twisted at her gut and made her double over in pain. After a moment, she inhaled deeply and straightened back up. Almost in slow motion, she lifted her hand from her stomach and stared. Blood. She'd been shot.

TWELVE

Pain was racing through her body, pulsing through her bloodstream. Inescapable, unending pain.

Someone nearby groaned. A deep, lingering, mournful sound.

Can't anybody help that poor soul? Doesn't anybody hear?

Anger swept over Amanda. *Somebody needs to help that woman.* She heard the pitiful, painful groan again and froze.

Heaven, help me. It's me.

She felt an arm slide beneath her back and another under her legs. She was lifted. Carried.

Ooh, stop. Please don't move me. It hurts. Please.

She wasn't sure if she'd spoken the words aloud or just screamed them in her head.

She heard two men talking but couldn't make out what they were saying. And dogs. She could swear she heard the low whining and woofing of dogs—or was it wolves? Had they returned?

She felt herself lowered onto a flat surface. Someone's legs braced each side of her. Someone's chest supported her back and strong arms wrapped around her torso, cradling her in soft, welcome warmth.

Dogs barked loudly now—excited woofs. Anticipation and energy filled the air.

"This jarring isn't going to be good for her, but it can't be helped. Hold steady pressure on that wound or she'll bleed out. Whatever you do, don't let up."

As if on cue, someone pressed something hard against her abdomen. She cried out and tried to skitter away from the pain but was held fast.

A voice she didn't recognize shouted a command, and she felt herself jettisoned forward in a jarring motion. The intensity of the pain as her body bounced repeatedly against the hard surface beneath her was more than she could bear. She didn't try to fight it anymore. She allowed herself to slowly drift away.

"Good, you're waking up." The sound of the woman's voice came closer, and Amanda felt a warm, wet cloth patted against her forehead. "You've been out cold for hours. I was starting to worry."

Amanda opened her eyes.

The woman looming over her looked to be in her mid-thirties with braided long black hair and mocha skin. Her dark eyes were warm, kind.

"Where am I?" Amanda asked as she looked around. She was lying near a roaring fireplace in a comfortable bed covered in a soft blanket of animal fur—bear by the looks of it. The one room cabin was significantly large and was divided into sleeping, living and eating areas by either small curtains or bookcases.

A huge, beautifully decorated Christmas tree stood beside the fireplace.

There were candles in the windows and the fresh scent of evergreen and something else…cinnamon… filled the air.

"Don't worry. You're safe here. You're in our home." The woman gently forced Amanda's shoulders back against the pillows. "Don't move. You need to rest."

Before she could ask any more questions, the woman supplied the answers.

"My name is Annie. My husband, Joe, saw a flare. He couldn't check it out at the time because of the upcoming storm, but he knew someone must be in trouble. He set out at first light and found you and your companion. You were both injured, so he bundled you onto his dogsled and brought you home to me."

Annie chuckled and held some warm soup up to Amanda's lips. "Joe knows if I can't fix it then it can't be fixed."

"Chance? He's alive?"

Annie chuckled again. "Oh, yes. It takes much more than a fall off a cliff and a bang on the head to take that one out of action. Although from the looks of him, he's had quite a few bangs and bruises lately."

Amanda's gaze flew around the cabin.

"He's out walking the perimeter of the property with my husband." Annie's tone sobered. "They are keeping a close watch making sure that whoever tried to kill you doesn't follow you here."

"Why are you helping us?" Amanda asked.

Annie blinked as if the question surprised her. "What kind of people would we be if we left two people to die in the snow?"

"Please don't misunderstand. I am very grateful for your help. How do you know we can be trusted?"

Annie smiled. "Joe is an excellent judge of character. He trusts Chance. I trust Joe."

"But you don't have any idea who we are. We could be killers or worse. And there's no one around for miles to help you."

"Are you a killer, Mrs. Stowe?" Annie asked gently.

Amanda colored, lowered her head and shook it side to side.

"I didn't think so." She leaned forward and fluffed the pillows behind Amanda's back. "Mr. Walker showed Joe his credentials and told him the whole story." She tilted her head and studied Amanda intently. "A plane crash, two and a half days in the elements, a pretty nasty gunshot wound and you're still with us to talk about it. You're one very lucky lady."

Amanda smiled but knew luck had nothing to do with it. She closed her eyes for a moment and offered a silent prayer of thanks for answering her prayers and keeping them in His loving hand.

She hardly dared to believe it. Chance was alive!

Almost as if he had heard her thoughts, the door to the cabin burst open. Suddenly he was standing there, filling the room with his presence.

Her heart leaped with joy at the sight of him. He was definitely alive, all right. He was banged up a little more than the last time she saw him, if that were possible, but nothing could steal away the rugged handsomeness of his features. Nothing could tame the wild beat of her heart when he looked at her with those dark, intense eyes.

Annie glanced back and forth between them, then pushed back her chair and stood up. She placed the bowl of soup on the table beside the bed. "Why don't I leave you two alone? I'll go see if Joe needs my help." She donned a heavy coat, hat and gloves. "Mr. Walker, please make sure she finishes her soup. She'll need the nourishment. You have a long trip ahead of you." Then she left in search of her husband.

Chance closed the distance between them, pulling over the chair beside her.

"Are you well enough to travel?"

The concern she saw in his eyes touched her heart. "I'm sore, but I think I'm going to be okay." She glanced beneath the covers at the thick, white bandage covering her right side. "I think somebody shot me."

Chance pushed his hat back and laughed. "I'd say that's a true statement. The bullet passed straight through and doesn't seem to have hit any vital organs. Annie was able to disinfect the wound and stitch it up. I must admit I was grateful you were unconscious while she did it, though. It looked like it would hurt a whole lot. But I must admit she did an excellent job. Bet your scar will be so slight you won't even notice it."

Amanda digested the information and nodded her understanding.

He leaned closer. "So? How do you feel?"

She placed her head against the pillow and thought a moment before answering. "Okay, I guess. Sore. Confused. Scared. But grateful the two of us are still alive."

"I don't know what frightened me more. Seeing you burst out of those woods right into a pack of wolves. That made my heart skip a beat or two. But I'd probably have to say the worst was finding you shot and bleeding to death after Joe pulled me up from that ledge."

He kissed her, this time gently, tenderly. "I thought you were going to die," he whispered, his lips moving against hers. His eyes glistened, and his voice held a husky note. "Don't you ever scare me like that again."

Amanda's eyes misted with emotions. "Me? Scare you? How do you think I felt watching you take a nosedive off the side of a mountain, huh?"

"You were scared?"

"You bet I was. It definitely took two or three years off of me."

"Only two or three?" Chance grinned. She felt his breath gently fan her cheek when he spoke. His rakish grin made her heart do somersaults. "Didn't know you cared, darlin'."

Amanda pushed him away. "Of course I care. I told you before. I need you to get me off this stupid mountain. It would be nice if you could complete the job in one piece, though. Don't you think?"

He laughed again, sat back and crossed his arms over his chest. "Yes, ma'am. I'll try to do that." He picked up the bowl of soup and held a spoon of it to her lips. "Annie's orders. Finish this soup. You have to get your strength up."

She slurped the soup as daintily as she could. First, one spoon. Then, another. The gesture was innocent and yet intimate. If Chance was going to continue feeding her, she'd drink a barrel full of soup.

"So what happens now?" And there it was—the elephant in the room. It was the question she'd been afraid to ask but now needed to ask. Would he finally listen to her side of the story? Would he believe her? More importantly, would he help her?

Or was she still on a one-way trip back to jail?

He stared at her long and hard before he spoke. He set the bowl on the table. "Amanda…" His voice trailed off as if he couldn't find the words he wanted to say.

She remained silent, giving him the time he needed to come to a decision.

She only hoped it would be a decision in her favor.

He sighed deeply, adjusted his Stetson and rocked his chair back on two legs. "The last time I let myself believe a prisoner was innocent, it almost cost me my life."

Amanda's eyes felt like saucers, but she knew better than to interrupt.

"Her name was Roberta Thompson. She was a very

wealthy woman…a young, very beautiful, manipulative woman…who had been accused of murdering her young son. She cried and begged and pleaded with me not to turn her in. I was young…and stupid. I couldn't believe anyone like her…with all her beauty and wealth…could possibly be a cold-blooded killer…especially of her own child."

Chance lowered the legs of his chair and leaned forward.

"I delayed handing her over to the authorities. I allowed my emotions…and my attraction to her…to cloud my judgment. As the days passed, I thought I was falling in love with her. She had convinced me that she was being framed, that someone else had killed her son and that she was heartbroken with his loss. I was willing to do anything to help her prove her innocence."

A cynical expression crossed his face. "I guess my biggest mistake was not telling her soon enough that her ploy had worked. She conned someone at the hotel where we were staying to smuggle her in a gun…for the promise of a huge sum of money, of course. And before I could tell her that I believed her…that I loved her…she tried to escape and shot me at point-blank range."

Amanda gasped.

"She almost got away with it," Chance said. "Except the person who smuggled the gun to her wasn't satisfied with an IOU instead of cash and decided to turn her in for the reward on her head instead."

The pain in his eyes pierced her heart.

"I was never that innocent or stupid again."

He stood up. "And then you entered my life."

The seconds ticked by, and Amanda held her breath wondering what he was going to say or do next.

"And you are beautiful…and wealthy…and convincing. And I can't help but feel déjà vu all over again." He stopped his pacing and smiled down at her. "Except for one thing. You really are innocent, aren't you?"

Amanda dared to breathe. "You believe me?"

"Unless you sabotaged our plane, hired another pilot to run me off a cliff and shot yourself, I'd say there's good reason to believe someone else doesn't want you to make it back. I can't think of any reason someone would go to all that trouble…unless they were guilty of the crime. Can you?"

Amanda's eyes filled with tears. "You don't know how much it means to me to hear you say that." She reached out her hand and clasped his. "I'm innocent, Chance. As God is my witness, I didn't kill Edward. Someone is framing me."

Chance nodded. "I know. And as soon as you feel strong enough to travel, we're going to try to do something about it."

Although Christmas was still seven days away, she'd felt like she'd just been given the best gift of her life. Someone believed her. Someone was going to help her, but not just someone—Chance.

She glanced at the Christmas tree by the fireplace and smiled.

Yes. *Christmas is God's promise of new beginnings.*

The four of them spent the rest of the evening talking and swapping stories in front of the fireplace. Although grateful that Annie and Joe had come into their lives when they'd needed them most, amid the laughter and camaraderie, she wished it could have been under different circumstances.

In the morning, after a quick breakfast, Joe and Chance set out one more time to make sure the area was clear. They'd decided last night that they would pack up the dogsleds and try and make it into Fairbanks later today. But they didn't want any nasty surprises along the way. So the two men set out for a small lake about two miles from the cabin. It was the only place in the area that a sea plane could safely land.

While they were gone, Amanda watched Annie pack supplies and felt a twinge of sadness. She hadn't had a female friend in a long time, and it felt like Annie could easily be that friend…if they'd met in another time and place.

"Are you going with us?" Amanda asked as she watched the woman gathering more and more items.

"Yes. Joe and I have been talking about leaving here and moving closer to Fairbanks. I guess this is as good a time as any."

"Really?" Amanda couldn't hide her surprise. "You're just going to pack everything up and move away from here? Just like that?"

"It's time," Annie replied. "Joe and I have lived out here for seven years. There used to be other families nearby. And all of us would get together every couple of months for a huge fish fry or picnic. But one by one they began to move back. We're the last ones. I know Joe loves the isolation…but sometimes it isn't good to be so alone."

Amanda studied Annie carefully as she moved about the cabin.

"We've been talking about it for a while now," Annie continued. "I want to be closer to families our age…to medical facilities."

Amanda grinned, suddenly thinking she knew the reason for the sudden move. "Can I ask you a personal question?"

Annie nodded.

"You're right. Towns have medical facilities...and other people...and schools. Annie, are you pregnant?"

Annie smiled shyly, nodded and Amanda believed she even saw a telltale blush tinge the woman's cheeks.

She clapped her hands together. "That's terrific, Annie. Congratulations!" Then she raced to the woman's side and hugged her.

Annie grinned. "After seven years, we thought this day would never come for us. But God in his goodness blessed us." Annie placed a hand on her stomach. "Children need to be around other children. We're not moving into Fairbanks. Living in the city would steal a part of Joe's soul. But we're moving close enough." Annie laughed, and the pleasant sound filled the cabin.

"What about this cabin?" Amanda asked, gesturing around her. "Are you just planning to walk away?"

"Why not? We're taking what matters most with us. Hunters can have the rest. Besides, we're going to need a bigger place."

Amanda found herself giggling with her newfound friend and wishing she could be around to see this little Alaskan baby.

A loud cracking sound wiped the smile off Amanda's face. Her blood ran cold. She recognized that sound.

The boom of a shotgun followed by the intermittent and distinctive sound of an automatic weapon spun Annie to face the foor. She pulled her gun out of the holster she wore on her waist.

Before she could move, the door burst open, and Joe and Chance rushed into the room. Joe paused in the doorway, aimed, fired his shotgun and slammed the door shut behind them.

"This must be the trouble you been expecting," Joe shouted across the room at Chance.

Chance, gun drawn and pointed for use, sidled up next to Joe. "How many of them are there?"

"Just one, I think, but one armed enough for half a dozen or more men, that's for sure."

"Have you seen him? Do you know where he is?" Chance moved closer to the window.

Joe gestured for the two women to get down and then turned back to Chance. "Best I can figure, the shots came from the woods on your left. I don't know what you did to this guy, Chance, but he's awful mad at you."

"I haven't done anything to him, Joe. He's afraid of what I can do to him. If I have my way, I'm going to make sure he's put behind bars for the rest of his life." Chance slowly raised his head and glanced out the window.

A barrage of bullets riddled the walls and doors. Pottery shattered into broken shards, windows exploded, showering glass and splinters of wood everywhere.

Both Chance and Joe opened fire. Within moments, the men were surprised when both women appeared at their side, weapons drawn.

"Amanda, you should be lying down." Chance tried to steer her back toward the bed.

"If this man has his way, I will be lying down—permanently. Let me help."

He stared at her, his expression pensive, nodded and then glanced at Joe's wife. "Annie, can you shoot?"

"You don't live out in this wilderness without knowing how to handle a gun, Mr. Walker," she replied.

Chance nodded and turned his attention to Joe. "Is there another way out of here?"

"No doors. There's a window in the back."

Chance sprinted across the room, shouting over his shoulder. "Keep him busy. As soon as I clear the window, the three of you shoot in the direction of the woods and don't stop until you're out of ammo or you hear me shout for you to stop."

As soon as he slipped through the open window, the three of them lined up where the front windows used to be and did as he had requested. Amanda was uncomfortable firing a gun. After all, she had only done it once before, when she'd shot Chance. But knowing he was out there with a killer, she didn't hesitate to place the barrel on the window ledge and squeeze the trigger.

The cabin was riddled with automatic gunfire again, the sound of it echoing all around her, hitting and destroying object after object until she thought she'd scream. And then just as suddenly as it started it stopped.

"Hold up," Joe said, raising his hand and tilting his head to listen.

The sudden silence was deafening.

"Chance?" Amanda stood up, peered out the window, searching the edge of the woods. "Chance," she called, again.

And then she saw him coming out of the woods, his shoulders were bent and his head was down like he carried a very heavy weight on his shoulders. She threw open the door and ran to him. She stopped mere feet in front of him, and they stared at each other.

"Chance?"

"I'm sorry, Amanda. He got away." He lifted his hat, raked a hand through his hair and put the hat back on. "I needed him for questioning. But I knew it wouldn't be wise to follow him when he took off and leave you behind."

"Did you recognize him? Have you ever seen him before?"

Chance shook his head.

Amanda held her hand against her throat. "Do you think he killed Edward?"

"I don't know."

"What do we do now?"

Chance stepped closer and wrapped her in his arms. "We go back to Fairbanks—and find that mistress you were supposed to meet."

THIRTEEN

Amanda couldn't believe she had come full circle. Only six days ago she'd been facing the end of her freedom, losing the last opportunity she had of finding the evidence to clear Edward's reputation and prove her innocence. Now she stood in the same bed-and-breakfast she'd been forced to leave, and for the first time, in a very long time, she had hope.

She couldn't believe how many things had changed in such a short time. Only days ago she had stood right here cowering from a bounty hunter, a man who had made her tremble with fear, a man who had held her life in his hands. Now he held her heart.

And Annie and Joe.

They had saved Chance and her from imminent death, welcomed them into their home and even came back here with them. They were helping Chance with his investigation by talking to the locals since many of them weren't inclined to confide in outsiders.

And even more than that, they were fast becoming good friends.

Everything had happened so quickly and so unexpectedly that it took her breath away.

Trust in God with all your heart.

And she did. Amanda knew she didn't always understand why God allowed things to unfold in life the way he did. But she knew he had a plan for her life. He could see the bigger picture, and that was enough for her.

Amanda had prayed for God to help her. She'd begged for more time to prove her innocence. But she hadn't prayed for this—these feelings she had for Chance were unexpected and maybe even a little frightening. She'd never believed she'd fall in love again. It was the last thing on her mind, the last emotion in her heart.

But she was falling, wasn't she? Hard.

Every time Chance came into the room, her heart skipped a beat. He filled her senses with his presence. And warmth rushed from the tips of her toes to the top of her head.

But it was more than just physical attraction.

Amanda genuinely liked and admired the man. The night of the aurora borealis, they'd sat together under the Northern sky and talked. They talked about their present, about their past. Chance had even told her about his father. He'd been raised by a man who lived to cheat and steal his way through life and, even now, cooled his heels in some prison for another scheme gone awry.

Yet Chance had devoted his life to doing the right thing. He'd proven his strong moral character over and over again these past few days in the most primitive and dangerous conditions. He was intelligent, interesting and had a sarcastic, teasing sense of humor she enjoyed. He was a man she could trust and depend upon.

But how did Chance feel about her?

Sometimes he looked at her with such intensity that she had no doubt about the thoughts and feelings in his mind. And his kisses were sometimes hard, demanding and other times as soft as the touch of a butterflies wings.

But at the same time, she strongly sensed the push-pull battle warring within him. He didn't want to have feelings for her—but he did.

She understood that push-pull. She was experiencing it herself. There was no question she was developing strong feelings for Chance. But at the same time, she felt guilty about having feelings for any man so quickly after Edward's death. And, she had to admit, there was an even deeper fear forcing her to try to pull away. What if Edward did have a mistress? What if she wasn't a good enough wife to keep a man happy, home and faithful?

Only time, and God, would determine how it would all turn out.

Amanda slid back the curtain with her hand and looked outside. The reflection of bright sunshine on the snow created ice crystals that glittered like millions of tiny diamonds as far as the eye could see. Icicles hung from the tree branches. And in the distance, in their breathtaking beauty and magnificence, loomed the mountains against a bright blue cloudless sky.

Somehow the snow, ice and mountains looked quite different from this perspective than they had over the past few days, and Amanda grinned, happy to be observing them from a distance in a warm, safe haven instead of up close and personal.

"Get away from there!"

Chance burst into the room like a gust of wind in a storm, grabbed her around the waist and physically moved her to the side.

"What were you thinking? Wasn't being shot once enough?"

His harsh, angry tone of voice gave her pause until she noted the paleness of his skin, the deep furrows in his forehead and around the sides of his mouth. He was frightened—for her.

"I'm sorry. I wasn't thinking."

He brushed past her and drew the curtains closed. "You can't afford not to think, Amanda. You have to be aware of your surroundings every minute of every day until we get this guy."

He turned and faced her.

"I understand. I'll be more careful." She smiled and started to take a step toward him when his expression stopped her. His eyes held an intensity that frightened her.

"What?" She hugged her elbows, bracing herself for bad news. "You're upset about more than me looking out a window. What's happened?"

"The local authorities are downstairs. They're talking to the owner of the bed-and-breakfast."

"Okay," Amanda replied. "They can be here for a thousand different reasons, Chance—including paying a social visit and grabbing a quick meal."

"Don White is with them."

Amanda raised an eyebrow at the unfamiliar name but remained silent and waited for him to explain.

"I've worked with him in the past. He's also a bounty hunter…a good one." Chance took off his hat and raked a hand through his hair before putting it back on. "Amanda, we've run out of time."

She plopped down on the bed. The blood drained out of her face. "No." She raised her eyes and caught his gaze. "There's got to be something else we can do. I don't believe God brought us through the ordeal of the past few days to have it end like this."

He lowered his gaze and appeared lost in thought.

"Did you check at the desk for messages?" When he didn't answer, she prodded. "Chance?"

He looked up and sighed heavily. "Yes. Apparently the message you had Joe post around town paid off."

"That's great." Amanda could hardly contain her excitement. "Did she leave a way to contact her?"

He nodded and held up a slip of paper. "No name or small talk. Just a time and an address left at the desk with this room number on it."

Amanda snatched it out of his hand and read it. She recognized the address. It was a small establishment not far from the hotel, a local bar and grill called Rhoda's. The note said to go up the back stairs and knock on the second door on the left at 10:30 a.m. She glanced at her watch. That was an hour from now.

Goose bumps appeared on her arms. This was it! It was the answer to her prayers. In one hour, they would meet with this woman, and she'd give them the proof they needed to end this nightmare.

Amanda chewed on her bottom lip and studied the worry lines in Chance's face. "I don't understand. This is the closest I've come in the past six months to getting the answers that will clear my husband's name."

Chance arched an eyebrow and stared pointedly at her.

"Okay, and it will clear me, too. So why aren't you as excited as I am?"

"Because knowing where and when doesn't mean we can get there."

"What do you mean? Of course we can get there. We have to."

"Amanda, someone sabotaged our plane, shot you and then riddled a cabin with bullets in an attempt to keep you from meeting with this woman. What do you think? He just took his toys and went home? If he tracked us to this bed-and-breakfast—and I have no reason to think he hasn't—then he is out there somewhere just waiting for the opportunity to finish what he started."

Amanda placed her hand on his forearm. "I've got you on my side. He doesn't stand a chance against Chance." She grinned at her play on words.

Exhaling an exasperated sigh, he folded her hands in his. "Go ahead and make jokes. If this was our only problem we might have been able to pull it off, but now…" His voice trailed off.

She pulled her hands away from him. "Don't tell me you're giving up—because I'm not."

"Don White is downstairs with the law." He grimaced and pointed across the room. "Just how much longer do you think it's going to be before they're crashing through that door?"

He caught and held her gaze, his tortured features looking defeated for the first time since she'd met him and her heart clenched. He was giving up. He wasn't going to help her anymore.

"I'm just one man, Amanda. I don't have eyes in the back of my head. I can't be watching for the shooter and at the same time be looking over my shoulder for the law."

Tears burned the back of her eyes.

"Don't…please." She held her breath and let her eyes do the pleading for her.

"Amanda…" His tortured look almost broke her heart—almost.

"We're so close, Chance. You can't give up now. Please."

He removed his cowboy hat in one swift, angry motion and threw it against the wall. He turned his back to her and just stood there with his fists bunched against his hips.

Amanda didn't move, didn't breathe. Hope is always the last to die, and she still clung to hers.

Slowly, he turned around.

"I'm going downstairs to talk to Don. I'll try to find out how much he knows. If he's sure you're here, I'll explain everything that's been happening. Maybe I'll try to talk him into going with me to meet with your mystery woman. You stay here, and stay out of sight until I get back. That shooter is still out there, Amanda, and for him it's hunting season."

Without another word, he strode from the room, slamming the door behind him.

Amanda remained frozen to the spot, staring at the closed door.

Stay here.

She paced the room. In less than one hour, she could be face-to-face with the one woman who gave her hope and possibly held the unwanted truth, as well.

Did this woman really know who killed Edward? Would she answer honestly about the "affair" she supposedly had with him?

Amanda stopped pacing and stared at herself in the mirror over the chest of drawers. Fear, worry and insecurity stared back.

What did this "mistress" look like? Was she prettier? Thinner? Taller? What? Would the woman be able to tell her what she had done wrong as a wife? Her stomach clenched, and the back of her eyes burned with unshed tears.

Stay here? While Chance and another bounty hunter went to the meeting in her place?

When pigs fly!

Amanda ran to the window, pulled the curtain aside and looked for a way to escape. It was a straight drop—about twenty-five or thirty feet. There were no trees to climb down, no awnings or shrubs to break her fall. She chewed on her bottom lip and stared at the frozen ground below. As much as she wanted to escape this room, she knew with certainty that this wasn't the way.

Amanda opened the door and peered into the hall. It was empty. Slowly, she crept to the top of the stairs. Voices…several, loud male voices…drifted up the stairwell, and although she couldn't see them, she knew the men were standing within feet of the bottom step. She'd never be able to slip past them unnoticed.

Trapped!

She paced back and forth in the hallway. She had to get out of here—but how?

And then she grinned.

The staff didn't use the main staircase. She'd seen them use a back staircase to bring up linens and room-service meal trays. It wouldn't be guarded. Most people didn't even know it was there. She grinned and started to run.

Chance picked his hat up from the bedroom floor only to throw it against the wall again—and again. He muttered expletives under his breath and then felt a sheepish wave of guilt. He offered a small prayer of apology. But somehow he didn't think Amanda's God would hold the outburst against him. After all, God and Amanda were on a first-name basis. God certainly had to know how frustrating she could be.

He planted his hands on the windowsill, stuck his head out and examined the ground below. The pristine snow showed no footprints or, worse, body outlines. At least she hadn't been stupid enough to try and jump out the window from this height. He closed the window, planted his fists on his hips and stared at the empty room.

How had she escaped? Don White, the sheriff and he had been standing less than a half-dozen feet from the bottom of the stairs and the front door. If she'd tried to sneak out, he would have seen her.

But somehow that's exactly what she did.

And it was just when he was pretty sure he'd convinced the lawman and other bounty hunter that he hadn't located her yet.

He raked his hand through his hair in frustration. He might not know how she got away from him, but he knew with certainty where she went. Unable to control his fury, he slammed his cowboy hat on his head and sprinted out of the room.

FOURTEEN

"Whoa! Hold up. Where's the fire?"

Chance had almost knocked Joe Hudson over as he hurried into the small café.

"Where's Amanda? Have you seen her?" Chance sidestepped the man and moved farther into the room.

"No."

"Yes."

Both Joe and Chance turned and looked at Annie.

"She came in about fifteen minutes ago and went upstairs." Annie looked at her husband. "You were busy talking to the man at the end of the bar and I guess you didn't see her."

Chance started to move toward the stairs, but Joe put a hand on his chest to stop him. "Wait a minute, buddy. I was just coming over to the hotel to see you. I have news."

"It will have to wait, Joe. I've got to get upstairs and see what Amanda's up to." He pushed past him and hurried across the room. "Why don't you and Annie have a seat? Order some coffee and breakfast…on me," he yelled over his shoulder.

When he reached the bottom of the stairs, he glanced at his watch.

It was 10:47 a.m.

He took the stairs two at a time.

Second room on the left. Second room. Second room.

Coming up to the door, he withdrew his gun, holding it down at his side. He paused and leaned his ear against the wood in an attempt to assess the situation inside. He didn't hear any movements or even the sound of voices.

He hesitated for just a moment.

What if she wasn't inside? He didn't want to blow the whole thing.

Then he grinned to himself.

This was Amanda. He should have known that nothing could have kept her away from this meeting.

He didn't bother to knock. Turning the knob, he burst into the room, gun drawn, and came to an abrupt halt.

Little surprised him in this job, but the scene in front of him froze his boots to the floor.

He lowered his gun.

"Amanda?"

She looked up at him. Tears flowed down her cheeks.

"Chance." She clasped her hands together in front of her. "I didn't do it. I swear."

When their eyes met, he saw a look of total despair. Then both of them turned their heads and stared at the dead woman's body lying on the floor at Amanda's feet.

The man stared at the cell phone in his hand. Perspiration beaded on his upper lip despite the below-zero temperatures outside.

This was going to be a *good* phone call. Now, if he could just convince himself. *Remember, good news.*

He pushed the memory dial.

It was answered on the first ring.

"Where have you been?"

The caller bristled beneath the angry censoring tone

but remained calm. He fought to put an air of confidence in his voice.

"I've been busy."

"It's about time." The voice on the other end of the line lightened. "Then I can presume my problem has been eliminated."

Here comes the hard part. A clammy nervous wetness pooled in the armpits of his shirt.

"Not exactly."

"Explain."

"I haven't been able to complete the assignment."

"Why?"

"Because she is never alone. First that bounty hunter was always with her. Now those two Good Samaritans who rescued them have joined the cause. Plus they've come back to town. There are people everywhere. People I know. People who would recognize me and be able to give an accurate description of me to the law."

A long, ominous silence filled the airwaves between them.

When the man spoke, his voice was soft, low and deadly. "Perhaps I made a mistake in placing this problem in your hands."

The caller's heart pounded in his chest. "I told you I'm gonna take care of it, and I am."

"When?"

"Soon."

"How soon?"

"Today. Unless…" his voice trailed off.

A low, controlled rage permeated the air.

"There's another bounty hunter here," the caller hurried to say. "He's got the law with him. I'm almost certain they are about to arrest her."

"Arrest her? And return her here? You imbecile. You

think this is good news? The only way I want her returned is in a casket."

"I'm going to try and make that happen for you. But just in case, I've done the next best thing."

"What would that be?"

"She's about to be arrested for murder number two. She just killed her husband's mistress. No one will listen to Amanda Stowe now no matter what she says."

Chance holstered his weapon and moved to Amanda's side.

"I didn't kill her. She was already dead when I got here." Amanda shivered uncontrollably. "I didn't kill her, Chance. I promise you, I didn't."

Chance grabbed her hand and pulled her toward the door.

"Wait. Where are we going?" She stumbled and righted herself as he dragged her across the room.

"Chance, wait!" Amanda dug in her heels. "We can't leave until we find the evidence she had. That's what I've been doing. I've been looking through the drawers, but I haven't had a chance to check the closet or her bags. Maybe we need to look in the room for hiding places, too. Maybe under the bed or behind a picture or taped to the bottom of the bathroom sink."

Chance stared at her incredulously. This woman watched too much television, and it was going to land her behind bars sooner rather than later. He took a moment to look around the room, noticing for the first time the open drawers and the clothes hanging askew from them.

"You did this?"

Amanda nodded. "I felt for a pulse. When I realized she was dead, I started searching. I have to find that evidence, Chance."

"Are you crazy? What makes you think there ever was any evidence in the first place?"

Amanda gestured to the corpse on the floor. "Well, someone besides me believed she had information. They killed her, didn't they?"

"If there really was some kind of evidence, then I'm sure the person who killed her took it with them."

"And what if they didn't? Maybe she didn't give it to them? Maybe they couldn't find it or didn't have time to look for it." Amanda grabbed his arm and tried to pull him back into the middle of the room. "We're so close. We have to look, Chance. There's something here. There has to be. Don't you see?"

He clamped both his hands on her arms and shook her lightly. "Listen to me! The only thing I see is *you*—a bail jumper, a person accused of murdering her husband who is now standing over the dead body of her husband's mistress. That's what I see."

"That's what you see?" Her lower lip quivered, but Amanda stood tall and stared him down. "Really, Chance? That's what you see."

He almost buckled under the pain he saw in the glistening wetness of her eyes.

"Amanda, please, listen to me. You've just left your fingerprints all over this room, and since you touched the body I am sure a good forensic team will find your DNA—a hair, skin cells, something on her body."

"I didn't kill her." Her voice was timid, barely a whisper and he could hear defeat in it.

"I know you didn't kill her." He put a finger under her chin and tilted her face so he could look directly into her eyes. He smiled down at her. "I know you didn't kill Edward, either. But if we're ever going to have the time we need to prove it, we have to get out of here. Now."

He saw a light come back into her eyes.

"You believe me?"

"I've just spent time in the wilderness with God's child. How can I not?" She smiled so brightly he felt like the sun had just burst into the room. "Now let's get going. We don't have a minute to spare."

"Are you sure about this, Joe? You can be charged with being an accessory to murder if you're caught."

"What murder? I didn't see anybody murdered. I didn't see any dead body. The only thing I can be charged with is helping a friend get to the Fairbanks airport."

He handed Chance the keys to a snowmobile.

"Leave the keys in an envelope with my name on it at the rental-car desk. I know the guy who works there. Annie and I will arrange to pick it up later."

"I can't thank you enough, my friend—for everything."

Joe slapped his shoulder a couple of times. "You just take care of yourself. Prove that little lady of yours innocent. And then come back and pay us a visit to tell us how it all turned out."

Chance nodded, boarded the snowmobile and slipped the key in the ignition.

Amanda hugged Annie tightly and then climbed onto the back of the snowmobile.

Everything was happening fast—too fast. Chance's head spun with emotions he had never felt before. He'd always prided himself on doing what was right, on following the letter of the law. In his world, there was right or wrong, black or white—no shades of gray—no concerns over whether the rules were meant to be followed. They were. Period. He had always found comfort in that.

He glanced over his shoulder. Amanda wrapped her arms around his waist and smiled back at him.

Now it wasn't so cut-and-dried. Now he faced shades of gray, and it shook him to his core.

He *knew* she was innocent. She hadn't sabotaged their plane or tried to run him off a cliff. She hadn't shot herself. She didn't riddle a cabin filled with people with automatic weapon fire.

He should be able to take her back into custody, explain the circumstances to a good lawyer and let justice take its course. He should be able to trust the system. He should… but he didn't.

All his values, ethics and beliefs were being challenged. He'd spent his adult life apprehending and bringing to justice those who thought themselves above the law. Now he found himself running from it.

Was it worth it?

Without a moment's hesitation, he started the snowmobile and sped away.

The plane was fueled and standing by. The bags were packed. If he left now, he'd be in Virginia well ahead of them. He'd have plenty of time to prepare a welcome committee they would never forget.

The boss would be pleased with him. He'd show he could think for himself—that the boss hadn't been wrong to give him the job in the first place. Nah. He'd fly in, finish what he had been paid to do and fly home free and clear no one the wiser. Maybe he'd even get a bonus out of the deal.

Throwing down his cigarette and grinding it out with his boot, he turned and headed for his plane.

FIFTEEN

Amanda stared out the passenger window of the rental car as Chance drove past a multitude of gaily decorated houses. Strings of white and multicolored lights adorned the houses, trees and shrubbery. Large inflatable snowmen and Santas waved from nearby lawns as they passed by. Grapevine deer with white lights intertwined in their twigs grazed peacefully on lawns. They even passed a couple of well-lit nativity scenes declaring the reason for the season.

She didn't need to supply Chance with her house number. Her home sat in total darkness at the end of the cul-de-sac looking forlorn and abandoned—in many ways echoing the feelings of its owner.

Chance slid the car to the curb at the beginning of the street. He doused the headlights and turned off the ignition.

"What are you doing? My house is on the cul-de-sac curve." She pointed her finger in that direction.

"Surveillance."

"What?"

"You're on the run. We have to make sure no one has been assigned to keep watch on your house."

His words caused the blood to drain from her face. *Oh God, please help me. Am I walking into a trap?*

Her eyes frantically searched the darkness surrounding her house for any signs of life.

"If someone is down there, don't you think they saw us pull up here?" she whispered and then felt foolish because she knew no one could hear their conversation.

"Yes."

"If we just sit here, won't it draw unwanted attention to us?"

"Yep."

The streetlamps and decorative lights threw enough light for Amanda to be able to make out Chance's features in the shadows. She studied the intense concentration on his face but remained silent and let him think.

"Edward and you haven't lived in this neighborhood for more than a few months, right?"

She nodded.

"Did you make friends with your neighbors?"

"No. Our work schedule and church commitments kept us pretty busy. Other than an occasional wave here or there, we kept pretty much to ourselves."

"That's what I thought."

The silence in the car became uncomfortable, and she couldn't stand it any longer.

"What are we going to do now?"

"Sing."

"What?" Her mouth fell open at the suggestion.

Chance glanced her way and then laughed. "What's the matter, Amanda? Don't you know how to sing?"

"Of course I can sing, but…"

"Do you know the words to 'Hark! the Herald Angels Sing'? Or maybe 'The First Noel'? We're going to sing our way down the street."

"What? Are you crazy? Chance, no…"

Before she could finish her protest, he'd come around and opened the passenger door.

"C'mon." He clasped her arm and pulled her upright. "We're going to stand at the end of each driveway, sing half a song and move on until we reach your house."

"This is crazy," she hissed through closed teeth as she tried not to stumble as he pulled her with him. "What if somebody recognizes me?"

"It's cold. It's late. If anyone pays any attention to us at all, it will be from a distance as they look out their window, smile and wave. Let's sing 'We Wish You a Merry Christmas.' You won't have to think about the lyrics. Now sing."

He opened his mouth, and a deep, rich baritone voice filled the air.

Amanda blinked hard and just stood there staring at him. She hadn't known he could sing. And he had such a pleasant voice, too!

"Sing," he commanded in a stage whisper. He tucked her arm in his, pulled her close and continued the song.

She did as he asked, joining her voice with his. But she had spent twenty-four hours a day for the past six days with this man. She recognized the subtle body language others might not—the tension in his muscles and the continuous darting motion of his eyes as he checked every possible hiding place, every shrub, tree or car as they slowly made their way from house to house.

He'd been right about the neighbors. A few had come to the window, listened, smiled and waved them on their way. Most ignored them.

When they reached her driveway, he seemed satisfied that no one was watching them and hurried her to the back of the house. She unlocked the door.

"What about lights? Should I turn them on?"

"We'll have to risk it. But I'm figuring there are so many lights on this street right now that no one will bother to notice a few more."

Chance followed Amanda through the small, quaint three-bedroom house, watching her as she turned on one lamp and then another. A large brick fireplace was the focal point of the living room, and he wandered closer. Framed pictures in various heights adorned the top left side of the mantel and drew his attention. There were several pictures of Amanda—digging on a beach, riding a horse, standing with a group of people outside an old-fashioned church with a tall, narrow steeple.

It was the wedding picture of Amanda and Edward that caught and held his attention. He lifted it from the mantel and stared into the happy, laughing faces. They looked like two kids playing dress up. Edward's blond hair was swallowed up by a formal black top hat one size too big. Amanda's veil was blowing in the wind. Tendrils of her chestnut hair trailed across her chin. They were laughing, young, happy kids and totally oblivious to how little time they had left together.

Gently, Amanda took the picture out of Chance's hands and stared at it.

"He looks so happy, doesn't he?" A puzzled expression crossed her face. "I just don't understand how fast it could all go so terribly wrong."

"Maybe it didn't, Amanda."

Her gaze shot to him.

"Just because you got a phone call from a woman claiming to be his mistress doesn't mean she was."

Amanda's lips curved in a soft smile, but it didn't reach her eyes. There he saw only sadness and resignation.

"You're forgetting," Amanda said. "The police found

a love letter to this mystery woman on Edward's laptop. It's what they used to establish motive when they arrested me."

"Like I said," Chance said and moved closer and cupped the side of her face with his hand, "it doesn't mean it's true."

This time the smile did reach her eyes.

"Thank you for that."

"I call them like I see them." He turned his attention to the photo she had put back on the mantel. "How old was Edward?"

"Twenty-five."

"And how long ago was this picture taken?"

"Valentine's Day. Hard to believe but it was only ten months ago."

"Edward was killed when?"

"May 7."

"In the three months you were married, did anything unusual occur? Did the two of you start arguing more than usual? Did you notice sudden mood swings? Unexplained absences? Secretive behavior?"

Amanda shook her head. "No. Not at all. We were happy. In love." She started to pace. "At least I believed we were."

"Then hold on to that."

Amanda stopped her pacing and looked back over her shoulder at him.

"Don't dishonor Edward or his memory," Chance said. "This picture shows a groom madly in love with his bride. And knowing you as well as I have come to know you, I..."

The air bristled with tension as silence stretched between them.

He took a step and turned her to face him. "I believe

the man loved you, Amanda. I don't believe he cheated. And if *I* don't believe it, then I think the least you can do is give the man you loved the benefit of the doubt, too. Believe in him. Trust him."

Her eyes glistened and she nodded.

"Good. Now let's get started. We don't have much time. I know this is going to be difficult for you, but you have to walk me through that night. Each step. Each moment."

She hung her head but nodded.

"Did Edward have a home office? Files?"

"Not really. We had a sitting room with a computer and books, which we dubbed our library. We both used it—me more than him actually. Edward did most of his work at his business office in town. His files will be there."

"Okay, then as soon as we've finished here, I'll want to see Edward's office. Go through his files. See if we can't find a connection to either of our pilots, particularly the second pilot Joe identified for us at Rhoda's."

"The police gave the key to my father-in-law when I was arrested."

Chance considered the information for a moment. "Okay. Then we go and see the judge. I want to question Edward's parents anyway."

"But…" Panic washed over her. "He'll have me arrested."

"I thought you told me that Edward's parents treated you well. That they accepted you into the family."

"They did."

"And didn't you tell me that Edward's parents were the ones who put up the money to bail you out of jail in the first place?"

Again, she nodded.

"Then we'll have to take the risk that they still care, Amanda. The judge will feel obligated to call the authorities…but somehow I think he'll do it after we leave. That little bit of extra time may be all we need."

"And if he doesn't?"

"Then we run." Chance grinned. "We're getting to be pretty good at it."

Amanda took one fast look around the living room that had once been her home…hers and Edward's. Her eyes lit on the picture on the mantel. So much had happened in so few months. So much was still happening and her emotions were spinning like an internal tornado.

"Amanda?"

Their eyes locked, and volumes passed between them without a word ever being said.

Amanda inhaled deeply, steeling herself for the ordeal ahead, exhaled slowly and walked to the master bedroom doorway. When she spoke, her words came out strangled and hoarse, but at least she was able to speak.

"When I came home that night, all the lights were on in the house. Edward wasn't in the living room and he didn't answer when I called his name, so I took a quick look in the kitchen. I called him again. I checked in the study and then headed for the bedroom."

Amanda stood in the doorway of the bedroom, her eyes glazed over as though she were viewing a scene in another time, another place. Her voice was husky, low and trembling. A lone tear slid silently down her cheek.

"Edward was lying on the bed. At first, I thought he had fallen asleep with his clothes on…" Her heart constricted with so much pain she didn't think she could take a breath. "Then I saw the blood."

SIXTEEN

A short time later, as they pulled the rental car in front of the two-story white colonial belonging to her former in-laws, Amanda could feel waves of tension pouring off her like steam on a hot, humid day. She sat so straight she might as well have had a steel shaft tied to her spine. She tried not to but couldn't stop grinding her teeth or wringing her hands.

Chance hadn't said a word since they'd left her house, but he'd glanced over at her a million times. She knew from the worried expression on his face that he thought he might be pushing her too hard, maybe expecting too much. They both knew that reenacting the murder scene at her home had taken a great toll on her emotionally. Now as they exited the car and stood in her in-laws' driveway, she felt the blood drain from her face and her breathing become shallow and quick.

"Amanda? Are you okay?" Chance's voice was soft and soothing, almost as if he was speaking to someone so fragile that any second they might shatter into a million pieces. She chuckled mirthlessly under her breath. Leave it to him to know her so well.

"The house looks beautiful, doesn't it?" Her voice cracked beneath her pain. Two huge holiday wreaths adorned the double doors. The entranceway was outlined with evergreen boughs. Candles shone in every window. Tiny white lights in all the shrubbery. And, of course, the whole house was bathed in floodlights.

"Anyone driving by can see how deeply grieved this family is over the loss of their only son, can't they?"

Chance glanced at the house and then back to Amanda, but he remained silent, simply arching a questioning brow.

"But shame on me, I almost forgot." She couldn't hold back the hurt and disappointment that clung to her words. "The Stowe mansion is registered every year for the annual high society Christmas tour. Open house so the not-so-fortunates can get a glimpse of the lifestyles of the rich and famous." She hardly noticed the tears streaming down her face. "Why did I think they would have declined this year? After all, Edward's been dead for seven months. That's long enough to grieve for your only son, isn't it?"

"Amanda. People grieve in different ways. Maybe your mother-in-law needed to keep busy to be able to cope with it all." Chance stepped closer to her. "Why don't you wait in the car? I can do this without you."

Her gaze locked with his. She knew he could see the hesitation in her eyes. She wanted to grab hold of the life-line he'd just thrown her and avoid facing her in-laws. It would be easier, less painful, safer.

Even though Chance made the offer, Amanda knew he would be disappointed in her if she accepted. After their week together in Alaska—surviving a plane crash, harsh elements, wolves, and gunfire, he'd think seeing her in-laws should be a piece of cake. After all, she was strong, determined and courageous. Right?

And that's exactly what she was going to be, even if she didn't have a clue where that inner strength would come from. She wouldn't take the easy way out, no matter how much she wanted to turn and run away.

"I'm going in with you. My in-laws won't talk to you without me." She shrugged her shoulders. "They might not talk to us anyway. They might just call the police."

Chance cupped her face with his hand. "Amanda, you don't need to do this."

Amanda took a deep breath. "Yes, I do." She whispered a heartfelt prayer, walked up to the front door and rang the bell.

Theresa Stowe opened the door and froze—didn't speak, didn't move, just stared at Amanda.

"Who is at the door?" The annoyed male voice drew closer. "Don't they know what time it is?" Judge Stowe strode into the foyer and skidded to a stop when he saw the scene at the door. "Amanda?"

Her eyes flew from one to another, understanding their shock and wishing there had been some other way to do this. "May we come in? I know it's late, but this will only take a minute. It's important."

The judge opened the door wide, looked back and forth to see if there was anyone else there and gestured them inside.

"Follow me." He led the way into the study off the foyer, crossed behind the desk and settled into his brown leather chair.

Court is now in order.

Theresa had yet to utter a sound. She simply sat down on the love seat on the other side of the room and stared in disbelief at Amanda.

"How dare you come here!" the judge chastised. "We post a quarter of a million dollars bond and you jump bail. Then you have the audacity to show up here…at my home…when you know there is a warrant out for your arrest." The judge reached for his phone. "I'm calling the police."

"Not just yet, Your Honor." Chance lowered his hand firmly on top of the judge's hand, preventing him from lifting the receiver.

Color heightened in the judge's face, but before he could explode, Chance said. "With due respect, Judge, please give Amanda a few minutes to explain."

Amanda's heart threatened to fly out of her chest as she watched the two men. They stared at each other in silence, seemingly sizing one another up. Then slowly Chance removed his hand and stepped away.

The judge leaned back in his chair, stared at Chance a heartbeat longer and then turned his attention back to her.

"Who is this man?"

"Chance Walker. He's a bounty hunter."

"A bounty hunter?"

Amanda nodded. "He took me into custody in Alaska and was bringing me back when…"

"Alaska! You jumped bail and went to Alaska?" The judge leaned heavily on his desk and sprang to his feet. "Young woman, have you totally lost your mind?"

"I can explain."

"Amanda, let me." Chance smiled at her and waited for her nod. Then he turned his attention to the judge. "Please, sir. Have a seat."

Chance filled the judge and his wife in on everything that had occurred from the moment he had taken Amanda into custody in the bed-and-breakfast in Alaska to the moment they pulled up in the judge's driveway. When he'd concluded, there wasn't a sound in the room.

"Obviously, sir, someone sees Amanda as a threat, and they do not want her to be returned to custody. Someone so afraid of what a continuing investigation might uncover that they are willing to kill to prevent it from happening."

Theresa jumped to her feet. "Is everything you've just told us true?" She stared hard at Amanda. "You didn't kill Edward?"

"No, Theresa." Amanda looked her right in the eyes. "I didn't kill Edward. I loved him."

"And you had found someone who could prove it but they were murdered?"

Amanda nodded.

Theresa's hands flew to her mouth, and her eyes filled with tears. Swallowing a sob, she ran from the room.

The judge watched his wife leave and then turned an angry gaze on Chance. "And you brought her here?"

A frown pulled at the corners of the judge's mouth and wrinkled his forehead. "We have a system of checks and balances, Mr. Walker. It's known as a court of law, and it was designed to provide justice. And we have lawyers who are deemed with the responsibility to make sure that truth is presented to the courts."

"I understand, Judge Stowe. And I agree. But we both know that sometimes the system doesn't work." He lowered his voice almost to a conspiratorial whisper. "I'm trying to help your family, Judge. I know this is a very sensitive time for you politically."

When the judge just glared and didn't respond, Chance said, "She's in my custody, Your Honor. And I fully intend to turn her over to authorities."

Amanda's heart skipped a beat, and her eyes flew to Chance. What was he saying? Did he really intend to turn her over to the authorities? Did everything that passed between them in Alaska just disappear like a distant memory now that they were back in Virginia? Or worse, had Amanda imagined that Chance had feelings for her at all? Had it had all been a ploy to keep her cooperative and calm until he got her back here? The thought turned her stomach, and she felt like such a fool.

"I don't think stalling for a few extra hours to give her an opportunity to find additional evidence can hurt." Chance leaned forward. "I believe Amanda is innocent, and I want to do everything I can to help her prove it. You put up the original bail bond. I'm sure, given this additional information, that you feel the same way, too. You believe Amanda is innocent, don't you?"

"Of course, I do," the judge sputtered. "But that's beside the point. Our justice department was designed to filter out the truth and provide justice. I can't condone this behavior."

The judge leaned his forearms on his desk, looked directly at Amanda and softened his tone. "I will do everything in my power to help you, my dear. You know that. I will hire the best attorney. I will speak as a character witness in your defense. But at this moment, there is a national warrant out for your arrest. I have no choice but to notify the authorities."

Amanda tried to hide the panic in her eyes and lowered her head. "I understand," she whispered. Her mind ping-ponged with multiple escape scenarios. She wasn't going to go to jail.

The judge gestured angrily at Chance. "What were you thinking? You know my hands are tied. I have to follow the letter of the law. What did you think I would do?"

Chance stood and stared long and hard at the judge. "I thought, because you knew she was already in custody and on her way back to jail, that you might be comfortable with giving us an hour or two leeway before I turn her in."

Amanda could barely still the trembling in her legs and didn't dare look at Chance. Was he telling the truth? Was he really going to turn her over to authorities? Would he be able to stand by and watch them put her behind bars?

"Why did you come here? What do you want from me?" the judge demanded.

"The key to Edward's office," Chance replied. "We need to check through Edward's files to see if we can make a connection between the names we came upon in Alaska with clients of his."

Amanda's throat closed up and she could barely speak. "I didn't kill Edward. Please, sir. Give me the time I need to prove it." She looked imploringly at the judge, held her breath and waited.

Silence beat through the room like a living pulse with none of them speaking or moving.

The judge opened the drawer in his desk, extracted something and stood. He held the key up in front of them. "Is this what you want?" He shook his head from side to side. "I'm so sorry, my dear. You know I can't give it to you. And you know that I cannot let you walk out of here. I must turn you over to the police. But I promise to help you…"

He placed the key in plain sight on his desktop and walked around his desk. "Now have a seat. I'll be back in a few moments. I need to check on my wife. You've upset her terribly. When I return, we'll call the police together and I'll go down to the station with you."

His eyes shot to the key on his desk and then he looked first at Amanda and then at Chance before he turned and left the room.

Chance grabbed her hand with his left hand and snatched the key off the desk with his right.

"What are you doing?" she asked as Chance pulled her across the room.

"Exactly what the old goat wanted me to. Now hurry. We've got to get to Edward's office before his conscious becomes too much for him and he calls the police."

SEVENTEEN

Two hours later, Amanda propped her elbows up on the desk, supported her chin in her hands and groaned. She glanced at her watch—1:00 a.m. She'd been officially awake for thirty-two hours. "I've looked at so many pieces of paper I'm starting to see double."

Chance grunted but continued to page through the files on his end of the desk.

"There's nothing here, Chance."

"Keep looking." He never raised his head or paused.

"But we've been looking for hours now, and we haven't found anything. No references to the names we have. No clues to anyone else who may have had a grudge against Edward. Nothing."

Chance looked up from what he was doing, and his eyes pierced right through her. His voice was deceptively soft. "What are you saying, Amanda? Are you ready to give up?"

Amanda's stomach turned over, and a shiver of fear mixed with despair raced down her spine. If she gave up, he'd have to turn her over to authorities. She'd be spending the rest of the night—maybe the rest of her life—behind bars. She broke eye contact with him and looked back down at the papers scattered across the desk.

"That's what I thought." He went back to the files in front of him.

They worked in silence for a few more minutes when a slight rustling caught their attention. As both Amanda and Chance jerked their eyes toward the doorway, the shadow of a man stretched across the floor.

Chance jumped to his feet. He reached for his weapon but froze when he saw the barrel of the stranger's gun pointed directly at his gut.

"You should listen to the little lady," the stranger said as he stepped into the room, slowly moving the barrel of the gun back and forth between them. "All of this was a huge waste of time. If I'd had the choice, I would have spent the last couple hours of my life in more passionate endeavors. But to each his own."

"Who are you?" Chance demanded.

"I'm your worst nightmare." His malevolent sounding laugh made gooseflesh rise on Amanda's arms.

The stranger stepped to the side and gestured them toward the exit. "Both of you head outside…nice and easy now. We don't want to get any blood on the nice office floor now, do we?" He scowled at both of them. "And if either one of you tries to run off, I promise I'll put a bullet into the other one's head. So think about that before you try any funny stuff."

Amanda's eyes flew to Chance. Slowly, he raised his hands and nodded at her to go first. She looked back at the stranger. There was nothing familiar about him at all… not his voice, not his appearance. But a sudden drawing pain in her side led her to believe she'd run up against him once before. Raising her hands, she slowly walked toward the door.

She reached the threshold, poked her head out and looked side to side for anyone she might be able to call for help, but the streets at this time of night were dark and empty. Her eyes flew across every surface checking for something, anything that she might be able to pick up and use as a weapon.

She felt Chance walking directly behind her, so close his breath fanned her neck. She knew he was trying to shield her with his body, and the thought of what might happen to him tied her stomach in knots.

"What's the hold up? Get out there."

The man must have shoved Chance with the end of his gun because Chance stumbled into her back, and then everything became chaos and motion.

Amanda fell forward. She stretched her arms outward to break her fall as she landed outside the front door and sprawled on the sidewalk. Quickly, she sat up and looked behind her. Chance and the stranger were locked in a fierce battle as they grappled for the gun. Their bodies bounced off the office walls, the file cabinets, the desk as the two of them fought for control of the weapon.

She had to help. But how? Maybe she could find something inside the office and hit the man over the head. The last thing she wanted to do was run back into the building. She wanted to run away...escape. But she couldn't leave Chance. He needed her help. She jumped to her feet.

Please, God. Please. Still need your help here.

She sprinted through the doorway just in time to see Chance seize the weapon and turn it on the stranger. With the gun in his right hand, he grabbed the man by the throat with his left hand and shoved back against the front windows.

"Start talking. Who are you? And who is paying you to kill us?"

A trickle of blood slid from the corner of the man's

mouth, and when he grinned it added a reddish tint to his teeth. "What makes you think anyone hired me?"

"Because you're too stupid to mastermind this yourself." Chance shook him one more time, raised the gun and placed the muzzle under his chin. "I'll give you five seconds to start talking or I'm going to blow your head off. One."

"You're a cop. You're not going to hurt me."

"I'm not a cop. I'm a bounty hunter. And if you think I don't mean what I say, you will be making the biggest mistake of your life. A fatal one. Two."

"You won't get any answers if I'm dead." The man tried to squirm out of Chance's hold.

"I'll let the cops figure it all out—after you're dead. Three."

"Chance, don't!" Amanda rushed into the room.

"Four."

"Chance, stop." Amanda tried to pull his arm away but it didn't budge.

The sound of gunfire froze Amanda in place. The stranger slid from Chance's grasp to the floor. She screamed until she didn't think she could force another sound out of her throat.

Time stood still as Amanda stared at the dead body lying in a heap at her feet. Thousands of tiny pieces of glass covered her shoes. Glass fell from her hair. Why was she covered in glass? And what was going to happen now that Chance had killed the one man who might have been able to help her?

Amanda reacted with a violence she didn't know she possessed. "Why?" She pummeled Chance's chest and shoulders with her fists. "Why did you kill him? He was the only lead we had! Without him we have nothing."

She hit him again and again.

His hands grabbed her forearms in a viselike grip as he ducked his head trying to avoid her fists. "Amanda, stop!"

She took one more look at the stranger's dead body and then collapsed in sobs against Chance's chest. "Chance. What have you done?"

EIGHTEEN

Chance wrapped his arm around Amanda's waist and pulled her with him as he raced across the room. Crouched behind the desk, Chance pushed her to the floor and placed his body between her and the windows.

"Keep down," he ordered.

"What?" She tried to sit up only to be shoved down again.

"Stay down, I said. The shooter may still be out there." Chance peered over the edge of the desk, his weapon drawn and ready.

"Shooter?" Amanda blinked hard trying to clear both her vision and her mind. "What are you talking about? You're the shooter."

"Shhh. Stay quiet and let me pay attention." Chance did a crab walk to the other end of the desk, paused for a moment and then raised his head over the desk for another look.

Amanda followed the direction of his gaze and realized that the front plate-glass window was gone. Nothing remained but shards of broken glass poking free of the frame.

She looked at the direction of the blood on the walls, on

the desk, on themselves and then it dawned on her. Chance didn't kill the stranger; someone else did.

She crawled the few feet to his side.

"You didn't shoot him?" she asked.

"Of course I didn't shoot him. He was our only lead." Chance turned his face to look at her. "You thought I...?" He shook his head and crawled across the floor to the dead man's body. Trying to keep one eye on the window opening, he started digging in the man's pockets. He pulled out his wallet, patted the rest of his pockets but didn't find anything else, and then he returned behind the desk.

"I can't believe this is happening. Who was that guy?" Amanda asked.

Sitting side by side, their backs to the desk, Chance opened the wallet and began examining the contents. He pulled out a couple of laminated cards and tossed them to Amanda before looking through the other wallet sleeves.

Amanda held up the card in her hand. "Jeff Lupine. Rhoda told Joe this is who hired Santana. This is the guy we've been looking for."

Chance nodded. "Looks like he found us instead."

"But I don't understand. What is he doing here?"

"He's here to kill you. Isn't that right, Chance?"

Both of them startled and turned their heads to look at the man standing in the office doorway.

"Now stand up. Both of you."

"Hello, Don." Chance nodded, stood and pulled Amanda to her feet beside him. "I must admit I'm surprised to see you here."

"Why?" The bounty hunter stepped over glass and displaced furniture and perched a hip on the edge of the desk but never lowered the weapon he held on them. "Because you lied to me in Alaska, buddy, when you told me that you were hot on her trail but hadn't located her yet? Tsk.

Tsk. Tsk." Don White shook his head. "That's not like you, Walker. You've always been a straight-up guy anytime we ever worked together. Why'd you lie to me this time? The finder's fee on this lady's head too big and you don't want to share in the reward?" He turned his attention to Amanda and grinned. "Or maybe it's the lady herself, huh? Have to admit she's quite a looker."

Amanda squirmed beneath the man's suggestive grin and scooted closer to Chance.

"Are you the shooter? Did you kill this guy?" Chance gestured toward the dead body on the floor.

"Me? No way. Didn't you?"

Chance shook his head from side to side.

"No?" The second bounty hunter, Don White, laughed loudly. "Wow, Walker. You're leaving bodies everywhere you go. What have you gotten yourself into?"

Chance frowned but remained silent.

"How did the pilot know where to find us? How did you find us?" Amanda asked. "And if you didn't shoot him then who did?"

"Ahh, good questions." Don White stood but still did not lower his weapon. He circled the desk and moved closer to the two of them. "Maybe he followed your trail from Alaska same as I did. Or…" He released a pair of handcuffs from his belt. "Maybe he listened to a police scanner just like me. Somebody called in your location about ten minutes ago." He glanced at his watch. "I expect the cops to be pulling up here any second now. And my-oh-my what a mess they're going to find."

Ignoring Chance, Don White stepped in front of Amanda. "Turn around. You're in my custody now. I'm going to turn you over to the authorities and claim that big finder's fee on your head, little lady."

He started to reach for her when Chance placed a firm hand against his chest. "Keep away from her."

Don White shrugged. "We can do this the easy way or we can do it the hard way…but make no mistake, we're doing it." He raised his gun higher. "You had your chance, buddy, and you blew it. Step away. Now!"

Chance glared at the gun, hesitated for several heartbeats and then stepped back.

"Look, Walker, I'm going to do you a favor," Don White said as he grabbed Amanda's wrist and fastened one end of the handcuffs. "As a business courtesy for all the times we have worked together, I'm going to give you some free advice. Take off, now, while you still can."

Amanda grimaced, and a low groan escaped her lips as the cuff bit into her flesh.

"Take your hands off of her," Chance demanded, taking a step forward. "She's in my custody…has been since Alaska…and I'm not sharing the finder's fee this time. Get it?"

Don White pulled Amanda in front of him and slipped the second cuff tightly around her other wrist, all the while gingerly holding his weapon on Chance. "She doesn't look like she's in your custody to me, buddy. The way I see it, this little lady seems to have turned your head. You not only *haven't* turned her over to authorities, which is your job I might add, but you seem to be doing everything else but turn her in. So I'm gonna help you out and do it for you." He pointed his gun level with Chance's gut. "Now move out of the way. I'm in no mood to say 'pretty please.'"

Chance glared at the other bounty hunter but moved to the side as instructed.

Amanda could sense the tension in Chance's muscles.

She could almost feel the anger emanating from him in waves.

"Let her go, White." Chance made one more futile attempt to stop him.

"Let her go? With the size of the finder's fee on her head? Are you crazy? The only one going anywhere, if you're smart, is you." White gestured with his weapon for Chance to move aside even more.

"Listen to me, Don. She's innocent. I'm trying to help her prove it. Help me and I'll split the finder's fee with you. Better yet, I'll forfeit the fee. You can have it all. Just help me prove her innocence."

"Really? You're a private investigator now, huh? Or a lawyer? Or maybe you joined the force when I wasn't looking? No?" He pulled Amanda closer.

"Bounty hunters hunt bail jumpers and turn them over to the authorities when they find them. You've seemed to have forgotten that, but I haven't. It's not our job to decide who is guilty and who's innocent."

"You know the system has its flaws. Mistakes happen. Mistakes that cost people their lives," Chance protested. "Someone is trying to railroad her, and she has no one to help her prove it."

"Breaks my heart, buddy. Really does." He shook his head and let out a low whistle. "This little lady really got her claws into you, didn't she? Too bad, brother. I hate to see the *second*-best bounty hunter in the country get torn up like this. Too bad."

He grinned at Chance. "Tell you what I'm going to do. For old time's sake, I'm going to turn my back for just a second and let you slip out the back. Cause the way I see it, the cops are going to arrest you for aiding and abetting a fugitive if you stay. That's if you're lucky and they don't hold the two dead bodies you've left behind against you.

How much help will you be to the little lady then? Now get out of here while I'm still being nice."

Chance hesitated, his eyes flying from Amanda to the window and back again. "Have the cops connected us to the woman murdered in Alaska?"

"Do dogs have fleas? That's what I'm trying to tell you. They're looking for *you,* too."

Amanda's heart clenched, and fear raced up and down her spine. He wasn't going to leave her. He couldn't, could he? She saw him struggling with the decision. She knew that Don White's warning that Chance couldn't help her if he was taken into custody with her was playing heavily on his mind. But she needed him to stay. She couldn't face this alone.

"Chance?" Amanda's voice croaked with emotion.

Flashing strobe lights filled the room as multiple police cars slid to a stop in front of the building.

Chance looked at Amanda, and the expression on his face told her everything. Her throat squeezed shut so tightly she could barely swallow. He was going to leave her behind. She could see the apology, the guilt in his eyes.

"I can't help you if I get arrested, Amanda."

"Don't...please..." she whispered.

"Trust me." His gaze locked with hers.

"Trust you?" She raised her handcuffed wrists. "How can I trust you?"

"This is pretty touching, folks," White said as he glanced out the broken window to the street, "but if you're going to make it out of here, buddy, you better hit the bricks." He gestured toward the cop cars and lowered his gun.

Chance ran to the window in the back of the office. Without sparing another glance at Amanda, he climbed out and disappeared into the night.

NINETEEN

A small desk lamp was the only illumination Chance allowed himself inside Amanda's darkened house. Since the office was at the back of the house and the curtains heavily drawn, he'd hoped the light would go unnoticed by anyone on the outside. He had holed up here for the past two days searching every nook and cranny for some clue, no matter how insignificant, to what had really happened that night to Edward.

He didn't believe that a young newlywed suddenly took up with another woman and began a secret affair. Everything he had learned in the past forty-eight hours from interviews he'd managed to conduct in the past few days with Edward's colleagues and past clients whose names he'd found in the office files, as well as the telltale signs he'd uncovered in Edward's home, painted a picture of a happy, outgoing, hardworking man of principle who dedicated his life to helping others.

Chance had made a trip to the mission where Edward and Amanda had first met. The people he spoke to told him what a great guy the blond-haired, hardworking young man had been. Twice a week, he had helped to prepare and serve the meals to the homeless, had rolled up his sleeves for kitchen cleanup detail and then he would sit for hours in the cafeteria offering free legal counseling or just company and comfort for anyone in need.

When Chance stopped by the church Edward attended, the praise continued. The pastor and several members of the church all testified that Edward had been a highly respected man of good character.

Even the neighbors living on either side of this house had told Chance that Edward was friendly, cordial and appeared to be madly in love with his new wife.

Although it was common practice for people to say only good things of people after their death, Chance found himself believing the picture everyone painted of Edward. A cheap affair would have been totally out of character for him. Besides, after spending time with Amanda in Alaska, Chance couldn't believe any man could ever want to leave or betray her.

Although that's probably exactly what she thought he'd done to her just about now.

Chance had asked her to trust him. He hadn't had the time or opportunity to explain his decision. And when he took the risk of being identified and arrested the following morning and went to the jail anyway to try and explain, she had refused to see him.

He didn't know what crushed him more—that her self-esteem would take a hit because she believed another man had deserted her or that she'd had so little faith in him. Either way, he knew she was suffering and it ripped his heart out.

Chance shifted uncomfortably in his chair and stared with unseeing eyes at the computer screen. His mind and heart wandered as he reflected upon his meeting with the pastor last night at the church that Amanda and Edward had attended. The pastor had been warm, congenial and more than willing to answer any questions or help in any way—unfortunately, he'd had nothing of value to add to the investigation.

But it wasn't the interview with the pastor that kept replaying in Chance's mind. It was what happened later.

It had been a small, community church. It looked like the ones he'd seen many times before in pictures—white clapboard with a tall white steeple. A small billboard, framed with evergreen boughs, posted the times of the services and events. A nativity scene surrounded by bales of hay and life-size plaster animals served as a focal point on the snow-covered lawn. Small evergreen wreaths hung with red ribbon against the white double doors. Glistening stained glass windows, drawing the eyes upward, flickered with an amber glow reflecting the candlelight shining within.

When he'd stepped through the double doors, it took a moment for his eyes to adjust to the change in light. As he stood in the foyer, he became aware of a delicate scent of burning candles tickling his nose. He moved into the sanctuary. Candlelight danced in lanterns every few feet and ended at the altar. Taller candles, remaining unlit, graced the front of the altar itself. The church presented a general feeling of warmth and comfort, almost like he was coming home.

His eyes had scanned the welcoming interior as he slipped inside one of the highly polished wooden pews. Bibles and hymnals were tucked into wooden sleeves in front of him. There was a piano and a three-tiered stand of seats arranged on the right side of the altar for the choir. The pulpit graced the other side of the altar and was surrounded by white and red poinsettias. And in the middle, drawing your eye to the center of it all, hung a cross—a powerful, impressive life-size replica of the body of Jesus.

Before he knew what was happening—before he could

explain it even to himself—he leaned forward and began to sob. His shoulders heaved and his breath came in deep, wrenching breaths. And he began to talk…just talk…to the God Amanda had introduced him to.

He told God about his life, his disappointments, his trials and, yes, his sins. He shared every secret thought and fear and begged God for forgiveness.

Please, Heavenly Father, forgive me…come into my heart and make me Your own…please.

It had been a heartfelt request, and Chance was astounded—and grateful—when an inner peace and warmth came over him, calming his tears, filling his heart.

Help me, Lord. Help me help Amanda. She's facing life in prison, possibly a death sentence…and I can't let that happen. Please, God.

He wiped the tears from his eyes, sat back in the pew and stared at the cross.

I can't do it, Lord, without You. Everything I do, everywhere I turn, is a dead end.

A slow, steady smile pulled at his lips.

But You can. If Amanda taught me one thing, it was that with You all things are possible.

Chance lowered his gaze, said a few prayers of thanksgiving and stood up to leave. He gazed one more time at the cross.

I know, Lord, that You answer all prayers. Just please give me the strength to bear the pain if Your answer is "no."

Chance had bowed his head.

From this moment on, Heavenly Father, not my will but Yours.

As his thoughts returned to the moment, Chance washed his hands down his face, ignoring the abrasiveness of a heavy eight-day beard growth. He looked at the screen saver on the computer in front of him almost as if he was seeing it for the first time. It was a picture of Edward and Amanda collecting shells at the beach, laughing, holding hands, the wind blowing through their hair, both of them totally oblivious to anything or anyone but each other.

No. Edward hadn't cheated on Amanda. Any fool could see just how much he had loved her.

Just as Chance had come to love her.

He had to find a way to save her. There had to be *something* he had missed. But what? He hadn't dared to try and go back to Edward's business office. After the murder of the pilot, it was an active crime scene.

The second interview with Amanda's in-laws a couple hours ago had proved just as fruitless. They'd been tense but polite and cooperative. The judge had been even more stoic and cynical after learning of the shooting of the pilot. But they'd let him in. They answered all his questions but, in truth, had had more questions for him than answers. They'd both grilled him for details about everything that had happened in Alaska.

Before Chance left, Judge Stowe reiterated that he intended to hire a strong legal defense for Amanda. Theresa shook Chance's hand, led him to the door and, after telling Chance she was sorry she couldn't have been of more help, she told him to offer her good wishes and support to Amanda the next time he saw her.

Another dead end.

Chance hit the space bar, pulled up Edward's email account and began reading the messages. The email at the office had been password-protected but this home computer had an icon on the desktop that opened right up. Unfortunately, as he scanned the emails, he understood the lack of password protection. He couldn't find anything sensitive, business related or helpful. He wished he could have had access to the laptop where the police discovered the email written to the "mistress," but they'd seized it as evidence.

Suddenly, Chance thought he heard a noise at the front door. He paused and strained to listen. He was sure he had heard the door open. The sound of footsteps against the tile in the foyer confirmed his suspicions and made the hair on the back of his neck stand up. He withdrew his gun, slid his chair away from the computer and peered through the crack in the open door of the study. When he recognized his visitor, he holstered his weapon, stood and opened the door wider.

"Are you looking for me?" he asked.

"Yes."

"How did you know that I'd be here?"

"Where else would you be? You can't get near Edward's office. Amanda's in jail and won't allow you to visit. If you are continuing to investigate Edward's murder, this is the only logical place to expect to find you."

Chance waited for something further, but nothing was offered.

"Why are you here? What do you want?"

Silence stretched uncomfortably between them as they stared at each other. Chance didn't move or push. His years of experience taught him that this was a critical moment, one that the person standing in front of him wrestled with, so he waited. It didn't take long. He saw the glint of decision the moment it was made.

"Here."

Chance raised his eyebrow in question but silently accepted the DVD.

"I'm sure you'll find everything you need on it."

Chance moved with lightning speed to the computer.

He pulled up the chair and inserted the DVD. He hadn't realized he was holding his breath until the file had uploaded, began to play and tension and air gushed out of him. He watched in morbid fascination as the "mistress," the same woman who had summoned Amanda to Alaska and had been murdered, paced back and forth in front of the fireplace in Edward's living room.

So Edward *had* known this woman. A slow, roiling boil raged through his body as he realized the impact this information was going to have on Amanda. He would have bet his last dime that Edward would not have done this, but here it was on video for the world to see. With a sigh of disgust, he adjusted the speaker volume and sat back to listen.

It didn't take more than a minute or two to understand what was happening in the video, and the impact of the realization pierced his soul.

Edward hadn't been having an affair with the woman. He was filming her deposition—a shocking deposition worth killing over. The woman became so distraught during the testimony that she asked for a short break and went into the bathroom to regain her composure.

Edward had left the camera on.

Before Chance could turn around and face his guest, he caught a furtive movement on the far side of the room in the film. In shock and horror, Chance watched helplessly as Edward was held at gunpoint, ordered into the bedroom, shot and killed.

Chance watched grimly as the killer wiped the gun clean and dropped it on the floor beside the bed. Obviously not aware that the video was running, the killer was about to leave when a scream from the bedroom doorway captured his attention. The "mistress" turned and ran for her life with the killer in hot pursuit.

And still the video continued.

It filmed the dead body of Edward Stowe lying on his bed.

It captured the audio of Amanda arriving home and calling his name as she wandered from room to room.

It taped the shock and grief as Amanda found her husband's body.

Chance's eyes burned as he became a silent witness to her pain.

As if in shock, she picked up the gun, stared at it like it was an object she had never seen before and then threw it aside. She grabbed Edward's shoulders, shaking him, screaming his name. She checked his neck for a pulse, placed her head on his chest and listened for a heartbeat. She frantically dialed 911 for help, hung up and began CPR. She screamed. She cried. She prayed. She begged, she pleaded. She did everything but the one thing her heart couldn't seem to do—accept that Edward was dead.

A lone tear slid down his cheek, and Chance thought his heart would break for the couple on the screen.

And then his eyes widened.

A police officer entered the room, quietly, gun drawn. He gestured for his partner to check the back of the house. The cop's eyes scanned the room as he stealthily moved across the living room. He spotted the camera, and it was obvious to Chance that the cop realized not only had the camera captured the entire murder but that the camera was still recording.

Everything happened in seconds.

The cop arrived at the bedroom doorway, took a visual note of the scene, assured Amanda that backup was coming and told her to continue with CPR.

He quickly slipped back into the living room and crossed to the camera. He pulled a cell phone out of his pocket. He forced the voice on the other end of the phone to state his name out loud so he could record it and then he named his price—a huge price that had set the wheels in motion that would result in two people dead and Amanda behind bars. With an evil, satisfied grin, the cop reached for the camera and the screen went black.

Chance felt a blow to his gut with the same force as if he'd been physically punched. For a few moments, he stared at the black screen, unable to process the horror of what he'd just seen, unable to move, to breathe. The blackmailing cop was the pilot who had tried to run him down with his plane, shot Amanda and now lay dead in the county morgue.

Why hadn't Amanda mentioned he had been there that night? Could she have been in so much shock she hadn't remembered? Admittedly the man looked different when he'd accosted them in Edward's office that night. He'd grown a beard. He wore heavy winter clothes and no uniform. But, still, how could she not have recognized him?

And then he remembered the shock, the horror, the grief he saw on the film as he watched Amanda fight with everything in her to save her husband's life. He was surprised she remembered anything about that night at all.

He slid the DVD out of the drive, slipped it in the plastic case and spun his chair around.

"How long have you had this?" he asked.

"About an hour."

"Why did you bring it to me and not the police?"

"Because I can't trust the police, can I?"

"I'm going to see Amanda. I'll make her listen to me." Chance stood up. "And then I'm turning this over to the authorities. But not before I make a copy and hand it over to the media."

A nod was his only reply.

"Are you prepared for the fallout? When I hand this in, everything you've worked your entire life to achieve will be over. Why are you helping me?"

"He killed my son."

Amanda sat in the passenger seat, her face pressed against the window, watching the festive house decorations flash by. She couldn't feel in a festive mood, even if she was fortunate enough to be out of jail—again. Her mind registered the lit lanterns on all the light posts through town, the myriad of homes reflecting white or multicolored lights as their decoration of choice as they whizzed past, but her heart felt heavy and empty.

Chance had run away.

She knew he hadn't been in a position to stop that other bounty hunter from arresting her. She'd seen the gun pointed at his gut and, certainly, she hadn't expected him to risk being shot.

But to *leave* her?

She could still picture the sight of him climbing out the back window and her stomach roiled.

How could she have been so wrong?

Not once but twice?

She'd believed that Edward had loved her, only to be confronted with the knowledge that their three-month marriage was a farce and that he had had a mistress. The pain of that knowledge had lessened over time, but it was still there.

Then she'd thought she'd found a second love…a man she could trust…a man she could depend upon…a man who had captured her heart and made her experience a depth of feelings she had never known with Edward.

Chance.

But had the feelings been real or just the manipulations

of a shrewd bounty hunter trying to cajole cooperation from his prisoner until he was able to turn her in? Had she misread everything that had passed between them? The feel of his lips on hers? The warmth of his arms around her?

She couldn't erase the picture in her mind of him climbing out the back window of Edward's office.

But she couldn't erase the sound of his voice, either.

Trust me.

"You're being very quiet, my dear. I thought you'd be happy about getting out of jail."

Amanda slid her gaze over to Judge Stowe in the driver's seat. "I am, Judge. I'm very happy to be out of there… and extremely grateful. I…I just have a lot on my mind."

The judge grunted. "Understandable."

"How did you arrange for my bail? The other inmates told me that if a person jumps bail they never get another chance. They rot in there no matter how long it takes to go to trial."

"That's true," the judge replied. "I had to call in several favors to make this happen. Matter of fact, more than my money is hanging in the balance this time, Amanda. My personal and political reputations are on the line."

"I understand, sir."

"That's why I'm taking you back to our house."

"What?" This was the first Amanda was hearing of these arrangements.

"Well, my dear, I'm afraid jumping bail made you less than trustworthy. Wouldn't you agree? This time you will be in my home where I can keep an eye on you just in case you get the runaway itch again."

Amanda sighed and nodded. "I understand, and I don't blame you. I wouldn't trust me right now, either. I'm sorry,

Judge. I know I put you in a precarious position. I won't do anything to let you down again."

"I certainly hope not."

"I'm surprised you're helping me at all. I know I don't deserve it."

The judge turned his head and looked at her. An odd expression crossed his face. "You're Edward's wife. This is exactly what you deserve."

Amanda offered a weak smile and said, "Well, thank you, again."

She closed her eyes and put her head back against the seat rest. "It's just that when that woman called she said I had to come immediately. She said I couldn't trust the police or anyone else around me."

"And you believed her?" The judge scoffed. "Sometimes neither you nor Edward seemed to use the brains you were born with."

Amanda knew it would be useless to try and defend herself any further so she remained silent the rest of the ride to the Stowe mansion.

Christmas was three days away—a time for family gatherings, celebrations and joy.

But not for Amanda. Her heart was heavy. All she could think about was losing Edward and then in her darkest moment to find—and then lose—Chance.

TWENTY

"The tree is magnificent." Amanda stood in the foyer and raised her head to take a closer look at the decorated two-story-high evergreen. "I hope it helped you and Mrs. Stowe cope with your grief. We both know how painful the holidays can be after a loss." She glanced at the judge to see his reaction to her words and then back at the tree. "You did a beautiful job decorating."

The judge grimaced and waved a hand absently in the air. "I don't bother with such matters. Mrs. Stowe is the one who tends to all that social nonsense. Here, let me take your coat."

Amanda shrugged free of the heavy woolen sleeves and handed it over to him.

"I'll hang this up. Why don't you go into my study and wait for me? We have some things to discuss."

Amanda nodded and walked through the living room and headed toward the judge's study. Poinsettias graced the base of the fireplace. Elegant glass balls were used as decorations on the various tables. Everything was elegant…and formal…and screamed don't touch or move in this room. Try as she might, she couldn't picture Edward as a child playing in these rooms. Nor could she understand how someone who had grown up in such a cold, sterile environment could be so warm and kind and loving.

But he had been that and more…and she was so grateful for the time they'd had together.

She paused in the entrance to the study. The interior was just as dark and forbidding as its owner—dark pine desk, black leather chair, dark pine bookcases from floor to ceiling, heavy drapes deflecting the outside light.

No Christmas decorations in here. No ho-ho-hos. No holiday cheer.

Her stomach felt like she carried a lead weight inside as she crossed the threshold to wait for the judge. She could just imagine what "things" he wanted to discuss.

A fierce, pounding headache throbbed behind her eyes.

Amanda wondered if the judge might have any over-the-counter pain relievers in his desk drawer. Sometimes she wondered if the judge ever experienced pain at all? He hadn't shed a tear when Edward was killed—not at the wake, not at the cemetery. He was the stiffest, most stoic, judgmental man that she had ever met.

She chuckled in spite of her headache and grinned. Maybe that's why he was such a successful judge.

And Chance was right. People grieve differently. She was being pretty judgmental herself right about now…particularly about someone who was putting their neck out to help her for a second time.

Chance.

No matter how hard she tried, she couldn't keep him out of her thoughts…or her heart.

Where was he? What was he doing? Had he been able to find any evidence to help her case? Was he even still trying?

She knew Chance had come to the jail and tried to see her. It had been her pride and hurt feelings that had turned him away. If she hadn't been so foolish, she'd have the answers to her questions and not be feeling so lost and alone.

Maybe the fact that Chance hadn't come to the jail yesterday, or today, to try and see her *was* her answer—one she didn't want to admit or think about.

The pounding behind her eyes intensified. She glanced over her shoulder at the study door and into the room beyond; there was still no sign of the judge. She didn't want to traipse through the house looking for him, especially when he'd told her to wait for him here. She'd made him angry enough. But she couldn't stand this headache much longer.

Amanda plopped down in the expensive black leather chair behind the desk. Maybe he'd have a bottle of aspirin or something in one of the top drawers. She reached for the top right hand drawer and then paused. She shouldn't be snooping in someone else's personal space. But an office desk wasn't really personal, was it? Not like a bedroom chest or wallet or purse. Besides, her head was pounding so much right now that it was starting to upset her stomach.

Hastily she searched the right drawer, then the middle and finally the left. She had always prided herself on her organizational skills, but the inside of the judge's drawers put her to shame. Everything was neat, labeled, stacked. Not so much as a paper clip was out of place. And, unfortunately, there was not a pain reliever in sight.

"What are you doing snooping in my desk?"

Amanda startled at the sharp words and sat back in the seat. "I…I'm sorry, Judge. I have a horrible headache. I thought maybe you might have some aspirin in one of your drawers." Even now, Amanda realized the foolishness of her quest. The judge had no feelings, either emotional or physical. Whatever made her think he might suffer from such a common occurrence as a human headache?

"You won't have a headache much longer, my dear. Trust me." He stepped into the room and closed the study door behind him.

Trust me.

Chance's voice, not the judge's, played over and over in her mind. She wished for the hundredth time today that she hadn't refused his visit. She needed to talk to him, needed to understand what was going on…needed to apologize.

Amanda started to stand and move out of the judge's seat, but he waved her back down.

"Sit. I want you to type something for me on the computer."

Amanda, puzzled by his request but ready to comply with his wishes, sat back down. She rubbed both her index fingers in small circles on her temple, trying to ease her headache pain, while she waited for him to explain. The sooner she got this task over with, the sooner she could find Theresa and ask her for some aspirin.

The judge crossed behind the desk, leaned forward and, after several keyboard strokes, loaded a blank word processing page on the screen and then stepped away.

Amanda turned her head to look up at him and smiled feebly.

"What do you want me to type for you, Judge Stowe?"

"Your suicide note, my dear."

Chance darted from lane to lane as he tried to make his way through immovable traffic. The roads were doubly crowded at this time of year, particularly downtown, with last-minute Christmas shoppers. This morning's light dusting of snow didn't help matters either as traffic inched

along, passing fender benders and slowed by rubberneck-
ers. He grumbled under his breath and honked the horn
to no avail when the car in front of him double parked to
pick somebody up.

"C'mon, come on!" He slapped his hand on the steering wheel, gritted his teeth and wished he owned a car that
could fly like in the old Jetson cartoons…or be a Trans-
formers tank that could flatten everything in his way.

When the older woman and all of her packages were finally loaded into the car ahead, the driver moved forward.
Chance took the first opportunity he had to pull out and
pass him.

It took him another twenty minutes to reach the jail,
five to park and make his way through the slippery park-
ing lot, two more to nod and make nice to the Christmas
carolers doing their good charitable act for the day that
blocked his path on the entry steps and then finally he was
inside. He couldn't wait to tell Amanda what he'd found—
correction: what he'd been *given*.

A small part of him felt sorry for the impending back-
lash of this gift—the scandal, the end of a political career,
the fall from social grace, the end of a marriage.

But his sympathy for the donor couldn't put a damper
on his excitement and happiness for Amanda. He held her
freedom in a small DVD in his right pocket. He hurried
down the long hallway to the sign-in window and could
barely keep himself from dancing along the way.

What if she wouldn't see him?

He laughed out loud. He'd make her see him. Period.
This was freedom day.

He skidded to a halt at the reception window, pulled out
his photo ID and asked to see Amanda Stowe.

The guard behind the glass barely raised his eyes from the newspaper he'd been reading. He picked up the license, glanced at it and then slid it back through the window.

"She's not here."

"Of course, she is. Amanda Stowe. Look again."

The man folded the newspaper and looked at Chance with a long-suffering expression on his face. "I told you, she's not here. I signed her out myself less than an hour ago."

Chance's mouth fell open and his boots felt glued to the floor. It took a moment for his brain to register what he'd just been told.

"You must be mistaken." The strangled sound coming out of his throat was a cross between a chuckle and a gasp. He gestured through the window to the logbook on the man's desk. "Check again. There's no way this particular prisoner would ever qualify for bail."

The guard was becoming impatient. "Look, I told you. She's not here. Judge Stowe signed her out himself. She left with him less than an hour ago. Now move away from the window. There are people in line behind you."

Left? With the judge?

Terror shook Chance to his soul. He was too shocked at the news to even notice that his first reaction was prayer.

Dear Lord, please. Be with Amanda. Protect her. And please, God, don't let me be too late.

He broke into a full-out run, heading back the way he'd just come. Screaming "excuse me" repeatedly as he barreled through the people in the hallway, he did not give anyone enough time to react. He slammed into the arriving visitors and tried not to bounce them off the walls or windows as he sprinted past. He skirted people, weaving in and out, like he'd earlier skirted cars in gridlock traffic with about as much success. He drew his cell phone out of his pocket, punched in 911 and wondered how in the world he was going to convince the operator that he wasn't crazy and she needed to send help. Fast.

Amanda stared at the judge and wondered if she had heard correctly. One glance at the icy glare he returned told her she had.

"I…I don't understand." She glanced from him to the blank screen and back to him. "What did you ask me to do?"

The judge tented his fingers and stared up at the ceiling as if he were deep in thought. "I believe the first line should read, 'To Judge and Mrs. Stowe,' don't you?"

She pushed the chair away from the desk and rose to her feet.

"If this is a joke, Judge Stowe, it isn't funny."

"Sit down!" Pure hatred laced his words and twisted his expression into an evil mask.

Amanda's body began to tremble. Her pulse raced, and her breathing came in short, shallow breaths. "I don't understand. Why are you doing this?"

"Start typing." The judge moved closer. "Don't make me tell you a second time."

Amanda slid down the back of the chair like melted butter. She pulled her seat up to the desk, placed her fingers on the keyboard and prayed she'd be able to come up with an escape plan. Or, at the very least, she wanted a way to stall him until someone interrupted them and she could get help. Deciding cooperation was the way to go at the moment, she typed what he had dictated.

"Very good," he said, reading over her shoulder. "Let's continue. Type 'I am so sorry for the pain that I have caused your family. I am so consumed with guilt for killing Edward that…'"

Her hands flew off the keyboard, and she dove out of her chair. She tried to make it to the study door but was stopped by a sharp, biting pain as the judge grabbed her ponytail, almost ripping hunks of hair from her head, and pulled her upright.

She scrambled to turn and face him. "Please. I didn't kill Edward, Judge Stowe. I swear I didn't."

"I know, my dear." He smiled at her almost sweetly. "I did."

Amanda blinked hard. She was speechless.

The judge killed Edward?

Her stomach roiled and a bitter taste of bile coated the back of her mouth and throat. She stared at him in disbelief.

"Edward loved you." Tears burned the back of her eyes. "How could you kill your own son?"

"He wasn't my son."

"What?"

"And Edward loved me so much he was blackmailing me."

Amanda wrapped her arms as tightly as possible around her waist, hoping to control the shaking that racked her body. "Edward would never blackmail anyone. Are you crazy? And what do you mean he wasn't your son?"

"Edward was a living, breathing reminder of my wife's infidelity. Every time I set eyes on him all I could see was her sin and betrayal. I hated him! I'm glad he's dead. My only regret is that I didn't do it years ago."

Amanda's blood drained out of her face. The shock and pain of this revelation was almost too much to bear. Edward had always felt that his father hadn't loved him. He'd told her that nothing he ever said or did was right as far as his father was concerned, and he could never understand why. Amanda had scolded him and told him he was wrong. Of course, his father loved him. But Edward hadn't been wrong; she was.

Tears flowed down her face.

Poor Edward! How horrible those last few moments must have been, when he realized that the man he'd loved and strived to please from boyhood was going to kill him.

"I don't care what you tell me, Judge Stowe. Edward didn't blackmail you. You're lying, just like you've lied about everything else. Edward had more integrity and ethics in his little finger than you can imagine. You've taken his life, but I'm not going to let you dirty his reputation."

"Edward uncovered something in my past. He confronted me with it and demanded I remove my name from the Supreme Court nomination." The judge moved around the desk blocking the only exit from the room. "And even that wasn't enough for him. He wanted more. He demanded I remove myself from the bench."

The judge threw his head back and laughed bitterly. "He had the audacity to tell me that he'd keep the dirty little secret. He'd let me retire with some semblance of dignity—but only if I was off the bench. He wanted to make sure that I could never misuse my power again." He glared at Amanda, and evil contorted his features until it was almost painful to look at him. "I could hardly believe my ears. The ungrateful, selfish, filthy adulterer's seed actually thought he was better than me. Talked to me about ethics and morality and doing the right thing. Well, I did the right thing. I killed him."

Amanda doubled over at the waist. She felt like she'd been physically punched in the gut, and she leaned heavily against the desk.

"Who was the woman who contacted me?" Amanda asked.

The judge flew into a rage. "She was a nobody that's who she was—a filthy prostitute who didn't deserve to live." He paced back and forth in front of the desk.

Amanda watched his every move hoping that somehow she'd find an opening and would be able to rush past him to the door.

"Years ago, when I was new to the bench, I'll admit that I found the power...shall we say...intoxicating? The harlot appeared before me on solicitation charges. In a moment of weakness, I offered to find her not guilty in return for certain sexual favors. That's what prostitutes do, don't they? Provide services that go above and beyond the standards of normal women?"

As he appeared to be remembering the things he had done to that woman, a sick, depraved expression twisted his features, and Amanda physically recoiled in disgust.

"So I hurt her. So what?" He stopped his pacing and stared at her. "She should have thanked me for what I did. She never had to work in her chosen profession again." He shrugged. "She couldn't even if she'd wanted to when I was through with her."

A slivering, snakelike trail of electric shocks crept down her spine, and Amanda thought she might vomit. What horrible things had he done to this woman? She could only imagine and had no desire to ask.

"I compensated her far more than she was worth for her silence. She lived off my money for years. But then she read the papers. When she realized I was nominated to preside in the Supreme Court, she tried to contact me. I thought she wanted more money. But I was wrong."

He threw back his head and laughed. "The witch had grown a conscience over the years. Can you imagine that?

She didn't want money. She wanted to stop my nomination. So she contacted Edward. She told him everything and agreed to testify against me."

The judge had stopped pacing and stood at the far side of the desk.

Amanda knew this would be her only chance, and she dashed for the door.

He was on her in seconds, his left hand digging into her arm as he spun her around. Without hesitation, he swung his right arm back and punched her in the face. Pain exploded in her cheek, and she could taste blood in her mouth as she fell backward to the floor.

Judge Stowe towered over her. He had composed himself and, for all outward appearances, no one would have ever guessed he had just ranted and raved like a lunatic and viciously attacked her. He smoothed his hand down the front of his shirt, patted his hair and then peered down at her as if he were sitting on his bench preparing to deliver his sentence.

"Get up."

Amanda cringed and couldn't help wishing the floor would open up and swallow her. If she hadn't been sure before, she was now. She needed God to come through with one of his miracles because she was about to die.

"You're going to finish typing the note I dictate. You're going to tell the world that you couldn't live with the guilt of killing Edward. You couldn't continue hurting the two people who stood by you from the beginning. You're going to sign it. And then you're going to blow your brains out." He reached into his pocket and pulled out a small handgun. "With this." He slapped it on the edge of the desk. "And then this whole miserable incident will be behind me. I will win the nomination, and I'll finally have what I've worked my entire life to achieve."

Amanda realized that it would be useless to try and reason with a psychopath, and it froze the blood in her veins.

"I'm not going to tell you again. Get up."

Amanda slowly rose to her feet. She glanced over the judge's shoulder. Her heart picked up a beat, but she kept her face expressionless as she saw the study door slowly ease open.

"Drop your gun, Stowe. Now!"

Amanda recognized the deep, masculine voice.

Judge Stowe swung around, started to reach for the gun on the edge of his desk and stopped in midmotion when he saw a gun pointed at his chest. He raised his hands and took a step back.

Chance! Amanda had never been so happy to see someone before in her life.

Thank you, God, for putting the right people in my life at the right times.

"I said drop your gun." Chance raised his weapon and moved forward.

The judge continued to slowly step back. "Let's talk about this, Walker. You're a bounty hunter. You work hard for your money. I am sure we can reach a financial arrangement that will benefit both of us."

Before Chance could reply, the judge's arm shot out and grabbed the gun on his desk. He wrapped his other hand around Amanda's throat and pulled her in front of him as a shield.

Chance, his weapon ready to fire, took aim. "Let her go, Stowe." He barked the order with a steel edge in his voice. "Or I'm going to put a bullet right between your eyes."

The judge pulled Amanda tighter. He laughed, insanity evident in the sound, and pressed his gun against the side of her forehead. "Maybe so, Mr. Walker. But not before I

return the favor and drop this little lady dead at your feet."
He tilted his head and studied Chance. "Something tells
me the stakes just became too high for you to risk it."

When Chance didn't move or respond, the judge ordered, "Kick your weapon over here. Do it now!"

Chance did as ordered.

"Good. Now step over here. Slow and easy. No tricks."

When Chance came within an arm's length of the judge,
the man pushed Amanda against him, almost toppling
both of them to the ground.

Chance regained his balance first and caught Amanda
against him, breaking her fall. Never taking his eyes off
the gun in the judge's hand, he pushed Amanda behind
him, shielding her body with his own.

"What did you do to her?" Chance spat out furiously
moments after he got a glimpse of the bruising on her right
cheek.

The judge shrugged. "Nothing compared to what I'm
going to do." He held his weapon on both of them.

"How are you going to explain killing both of us?"
Amanda asked. "No one is going to believe a double suicide."

"You underestimate me, my dear. I have the scenario
already planned out." He gestured with the gun moving
them back against the wall.

"When Mr. Walker discovered I had arranged to bail
you out a second time, he felt I was in danger. He rushed
to my home to tell me me that you had confessed to killing
Edward when you were stranded with him in Alaska and
he planned on testifying against you. When we confronted
you in the study with the new information, we discovered
you had already typed a suicide note. You shot Mr. Walker
before he could stop you from harming yourself and then
turned the weapon on yourself."

The judge shrugged. "It might take a little persuasion, a bit of acting perhaps, but I'm not worried. Everyone knows who I am. I have a stellar reputation in this community. I am a nominee for the highest court in the land. And you, my dear? You're a murderess. You have left a trail of bodies from here to Alaska and back again. In the end, who do you think people will believe?"

A slow, satisfied grin pulled at his lips.

"Now whisper your goodbyes to each other." He raised his weapon, aimed and the sound of gunfire filled the air.

The judge grimaced. He had been shot in the arm. Instantly, he swung toward the doorway and returned fire.

Chance leaped on top of the judge's back, and both of them crashed to the floor. They struggled, rolling back and forth on the carpet, punching each other, pulling and pushing for control of the gun.

When the sound of a second blast filled the room, Amanda froze. Who had been shot…Chance or the judge? She stared at the two men still entangled on the floor and felt like her heart was being squeezed in a giant vise. When Chance pushed himself into a sitting position, a prayer of gratitude formed on her lips, and she breathed a sigh of relief.

The judge groaned. A bright red spot spread across the left side of his chest. Without ever opening his eyes or saying another word, he placed his arms at his sides and died.

Chance leaned over to check for a pulse.

Amanda rushed past him to the doorway to see who the judge had shot. She cried out and raced to the woman's side. Kneeling beside her mother-in-law, she felt a horrible sense of déjà vu. She deftly examined the gunshot wound in her chest. It appeared to be the same kind of injury that had claimed Edward's life that horrible night. Fear for the woman shivered through her veins.

"Theresa, I'm so sorry." She placed the heel of her hand against the woman's breast, applied pressure and screamed for Chance to call 911.

Theresa smiled feebly at her. "Shh, don't bother, child. There's nothing anyone can do."

Although Theresa had not been able to hide her disappointment that Edward had married "beneath his social standing," her mother-in-law had always treated her with respect and kindness, even affection from time to time. Amanda had to admit that she had grown fond of Edward's mother, too.

When Edward was killed, Theresa had refused to even entertain the possibility that Amanda had killed him. Her emotional support had meant so much. As she gazed down at her mother-in-law now, she felt a deep, soul-penetrating sadness wash over her.

"You're going to be all right, Theresa." The distant wail of sirens grew louder. Amanda smoothed back Theresa's hair. "Hear that? The EMTs will be pulling up outside any minute now. You have to hold on." She kept pressure on the wound with her left hand. Leaning over, she lightly kissed the older woman's forehead. "Please, Theresa. Don't give up."

Theresa looked directly into her eyes.

"I should have left him right after Edward was born."

"Why didn't you?" Amanda asked. "I can't imagine how hard it must have been for you to live with a man who harbored such anger and bitterness."

"I deserved it. I betrayed him. He had a right to be angry and bitter."

"No one deserves a life of punishment by another human being. God is our only judge, Theresa."

"I stayed for Edward. My husband agreed to provide Edward with the best of everything...the finest schools money could buy. In return, I stayed with him, covered up the scandal my behavior would have caused, helped him socially build his power." Theresa let a tear slide down her cheek.

Amanda's heart filled with pain when she realized that Theresa had spent her entire life pursuing material things that, in the end, didn't matter and missing out on the precious things in life that did.

"Would you like me to say a prayer with you?"

Theresa nodded, and Amanda bowed her head and prayed...for forgiveness...for peace. A comfortable silence...a bonding they hadn't been able to form in the short months before...enveloped them.

"I need you to listen to me." Theresa grasped Amanda's hand. "I need to make you understand." A frantic look came into her eyes, and she seemed to be getting agitated.

"Shh, Theresa. Don't worry. I'm right here. I'm not going anywhere. Conserve your strength. You can tell me whatever you need to say when we get you to the hospital. Okay?"

"No!" She became even more forceful and stressed. "Now!" The woman tried to sit up but the effort was too much for her.

Amanda slid her arm beneath the older woman's shoulder and cradled her upper body in her arms. "Theresa, please. Calm down. I'm listening."

Theresa gazed up at Amanda and nodded.

"Don't you believe those vicious lies." She coughed violently, and the physical exertion made her gasp for air. When she had caught her breath, she looked once more at Amanda. "Edward loved you—with all his heart. I could hear the happiness in his voice when he talked to me about you—I saw such joy in his eyes..."

The older woman had another coughing spasm but forced herself to continue. "There never was another woman. Only you. Never forget that." She squeezed Amanda's hand. "Promise me."

Amanda, her throat too constricted to speak, simply nodded and smiled lovingly at the older woman.

Theresa returned a weak smile and took her last breath.

TWENTY-ONE

A deep chill seeped through every pore in Amanda's body and seemed to wrap tentacles around her bones. Even though she stood in the well-heated foyer of the Stowe mansion and not outside in the frigid air, she couldn't seem to get warm. Even her teeth clattered together. A distant voice whispered in the recesses of her mind that she must be in shock. She didn't care whether she was in shock or not. She just wanted to stop shaking.

Amanda tried to ignore the parade of law-enforcement officials and forensic workers who had scurried in and out of the house over the past hour. She grimaced and turned away at the sight of the body finally being moved out of the library and couldn't help but wonder who rested beneath the dark plastic...the judge or his wife?

Her eyes pooled with tears as she thought about her last moments with Theresa and, unable to deal with her emotions, she turned her back as the gurney passed.

Amanda's eyes wandered over the two-story-high Christmas tree in the foyer, and her thoughts turned to Edward. This would have been their first Christmas together, she and Edward, as a married couple. A small part of her was grateful that he had been spared the pain of seeing what had happened to his family.

She raised her eyes to the shiny star on the top of the tree. What had she told Chance when they'd crashed in Alaska? Christmas is a time of hope, God's promise of new beginnings.

Amanda startled as a blanket was placed over her shoulders and two strong arms wrapped it around her.

"Are you okay?"

Chance's deep, comforting voice sounded beside her left ear, his lips tickling her skin, his breath a whisper of warmth. "I spoke with the district attorney. He's almost finished in the judge's study. He watched the DVD. He assured me that once he has a chance to formally review the new evidence that he expects to drop all the charges against you."

He released his hold on her blanket, dropping his arms to his side, and Amanda felt like all the warmth and safety in the room moved away with him. She wanted to turn and throw herself into his arms. She wanted to cling to him, bury her face in the rock hard wall of his chest, feel his arms cradle her against him like he'd done in the snowy Alaskan wilderness. She wanted to cry…and smile…and hope, but she didn't move. She stood motionless, waiting. But for what she wasn't sure.

"I also spoke with the sheriff." The sound of Chance's voice had moved back with him. She no longer felt his lips against her skin, no longer felt his breath whisper through her hair and a deep, undefined sadness touched her soul. What was going to happen now? What was going to happen to them? Had there ever even been a "them"?

"He said that it's okay for you to leave. He's got some questions for you, but he'll contact you later." Chance turned her to face him and tilted her face with his index finger. "Hey, are you all right?"

She stared deeply into the dark eyes looking back at her,

and she didn't want the moment to pass. She didn't want to know the answer to her questions—probably because she was afraid of what those answers might be.

"There are still some things I don't understand." She gazed up at him. "You told me that the pilot who tried to kill us was a dirty cop? That he saw an opportunity to blackmail the judge and took it."

Chance nodded. "But I think he got much more than he bargained for. When he first blackmailed the judge, he hadn't seen the tape. He just assumed it had recorded you murdering your husband and he figured he could make a sizable sum by keeping it out of the judge's headlines."

Chance shook his head. "I can only imagine how surprised he was when he did watch the tape and discovered the judge was the murderer. He must have realized then that he was in over his head, but it was too late. He took his money and got as far away from the judge as he could."

Chance shrugged. "It probably worked for a while. But blackmailing the judge had actually put him right in the judge's back pocket. He couldn't afford to say 'no' when the judge asked for his help."

"I want to watch the DVD," Amanda said.

"What?" A frown creased his mouth and deep lines formed in his forehead.

"You said the DVD showed without a doubt that the judge killed Edward. I want to see for myself."

Chance reached out and stroked the sides of her arms. His voice was steady but firm. "No. You don't."

Amanda's eyes filled with tears. "Those were Edward's last moments on this earth. I want to see it. I have a right to see it. I was his wife." She heard the hysteria in her voice but could do nothing to control it.

"Amanda." Chance clasped her arms tightly, and he pulled her closer to him. He looked down into her face, and all she could see was compassion. "You don't want to see the video. You don't want to remember Edward that way. And I'm pretty sure if Edward were here he would say the same thing to you."

He smiled down at her. "If you want to remember something, remember his laughter. Remember those two kids in that wedding picture. Remember the last time he kissed you or even the last words he said before you left the house that night. But for both of your sakes...don't print an indelible picture on your mind of his death. I don't believe he would have wanted that for you. Do you?"

She hesitated, her mind already flashing to the sight of Edward lying motionless on the bed...memories of blood...of panic...of despair and pain.

Slowly, she shook her head. When she thought of Edward, her heart mourned the loss of the idealistic young man who was going to help save the world.

"No. You're right," she said, her voice a mere whisper. "I want to remember Edward grinning ear to ear when he won a case for an innocent person or how he joked and smiled with the people as he dished out food to the homeless at the mission." A lone tear slid down her cheek. "That was Edward. That was the man I will always remember." She smiled up at Chance. "You would have liked him, you know."

"I'm sure I would have," Chance said and he meant it. He hugged her briefly. "Now why don't you let me drive you home."

Home?

Where was home? An empty, dark house where her husband had been murdered?

Isn't home supposed to be where your heart is?

Mental images flooded her mind of a plane wreckage on an Alaskan mountain, of roaring fires, the aurora borealis, the poor excuse of a scrawny branch pretending to be a Christmas tree. She remembered dogsled rides and a cozy cabin in the woods, new friends and a particular bed-and-breakfast. Alaska—where she'd fallen in love... maybe the first real, grown-up love she'd ever known.

And now?

She glanced up at Chance, moved by the deep concern she saw in those dark compelling eyes. Without another word, he clasped her elbow and steered her toward the door.

They drove in silence, an unspoken tension in the air between them, and they didn't speak again until they pulled up outside the dark, empty house at the back of the cul-de-sac.

Chance came around the car, opened the passenger door and walked with her to the front door.

"Give me your key. I'll turn on a few lights and make sure everything's okay." He took the key from her hand, unlocked and opened the door and disappeared inside.

Amanda stepped inside and slowly removed her scarf and coat while lights clicked on throughout the house and she waited for Chance to return.

Within minutes, he'd kept his word, strode through the house to make sure all was safe and returned to stand beside her at the front door.

He placed the key in her hand, his fingers lingering their hold of her hand a moment longer than necessary... and then his hand fell away.

"I made a quick sweep of the house, and everything seems to be in order. I turned the thermostat up in the hallway. It should warm up in here shortly."

"Thanks. I appreciate it." She busied herself with hanging up her coat in the hall closet. "Would you like a cup of coffee?" she called over her shoulder.

"No. I really should be going."

She nodded as she stepped back into the entranceway. "I understand."

"Would you like me to start a fire for you before I leave?"

"No." She wrapped her arms around her body. "I'll be fine."

An uncomfortable tension grew between them.

Amanda stared at the diamond pattern of the tiled floor. She didn't dare look up at Chance. She knew she couldn't hide her feelings from him any longer…that her expression would tell him everything her words couldn't say… that her eyes would shine with her newly discovered love for this mountain of a man.

So she waited for him to make the first move…or say the first word…or let her know in any way that it wasn't her imagination, that their time together had meant as much to him as it had to her.

She held her breath…and hoped…and prayed.

"The sheriff said he'd call you tomorrow," Chance reminded her. "He still has a few questions, but I convinced him they could wait until morning."

She smiled and nodded.

"Well…I guess I should be going."

Amanda's heart pounded in her chest.

Going? No! She couldn't let him go—not after everything they'd been through together. She couldn't let him go now or ever.

Her eyes flew to his.

"Chance…" She whispered his name and knew that all her emotions laced that simple word.

He stepped close…so close.

She could feel the heat from his body. His dark eyes

locked and held her gaze…saying everything, saying nothing.

Ever so slowly he lowered his head and pressed his lips against hers. Gently. Tenderly. Barely touching skin to skin. He lifted his face mere inches from hers and stared at her with an intensity she couldn't read and didn't understand.

"Chance?" she whispered again.

"You're free now, Amanda. You're safe." He stepped away from her. "Try and get some rest."

A mask fell over his expression, and Amanda suddenly felt cold and alone. How many times can a heart break before a person doesn't have a heart anymore, she wondered? He didn't have to say it. It was written all over him. He was leaving her. Their Alaska adventure had ended… they had ended.

"Good night, Amanda."

She wrapped her arms tighter around her body and simply nodded.

Then, just like that, he was gone.

Chance Walker pounded his fist against the steering wheel of his car as he drove away. He swiped at the sudden wetness on his face and was surprised to find tears running down his cheeks. What was happening to him? The first time he'd shed tears since he'd been a boy was in church…and now?

But the pain of leaving Amanda was so intense…how could he not cry?

He pulled onto the freeway and tried to concentrate on his driving. He was grateful the hour was late and there weren't many cars on the road.

It had almost killed him to leave her. He had wanted

to tell her how much she meant to him. He had wanted to wrap her in his arms and never let her go.

But that wouldn't have been fair to Amanda.

He needed to give her time to process everything that had happened to her. She was a young widow who had just been cleared of her husband's murder. She had just lost the only mother figure she'd had since childhood. She still faced the formality of questions and paperwork before she'd formally clear her name and gain her freedom.

She'd been through so much in such a short period of time that he knew her head and her heart would be spinning. He couldn't dump his feelings on her now—not if he truly loved her and he did. Lord help him, but he loved her with every fiber of his being.

So he'd give her time.

It was time to celebrate her hard-won freedom. It was time to deal with her grief for a young lost love. It was time to sort through her own feelings and make sense of what had happened between the two of them. It was time to clarify in her own mind what exactly…if anything… she felt for him.

He knew something special—something strong and real had blossomed between them out there in God's country. All she needed was rest—to heal, to remember.

And then he'd tell her what was in his heart. And she'd listen. And she'd love him back. Wouldn't she?

As his car continued down the darkened highway, he began to pray.

Christmas morning had come and gone like any other morning. She'd fixed her coffee and forced herself to eat a slice of toast. She'd gazed out the window and watched the neighborhood children play with the new sleds that Santa must have brought. She'd sat in front of the fire in the fireplace and looked through old photo albums. She'd said her prayers and done her Bible study and remembered the reason for the season—the promise of God with us. She allowed herself to feel gratitude...and hope.

As daylight slipped into twilight and shadows stretched across the living room floor, she tried not to let her eyes stray to the telephone, but it was hopeless. She'd stared at that phone for three days, ever since Chance left, and wished a million times for it to ring. So much for mental telepathy.

She fixed herself a sandwich and a mug of hot chocolate, and as twilight eased into darkness, she decided to turn in early and try to get some sleep—something she'd had very little of lately. Maybe things would look better in the morning, if she could just stop crying and get through Christmas—alone.

She reached out to turn off the living room light when the doorbell rang.

Amanda pulled back the curtain and peeked outside. Her heart skipped a beat, and she forced herself not to run to the door and throw herself in his arms.

Be calm. Be cordial. Don't make a fool of yourself. See why he's here.

Please, God. Let him be here for the right reasons.

Amanda couldn't seem to unlock the dead bolt fast enough. She swung the door open wide and couldn't contain the grin that burst wide on her face.

"Merry Christmas, Chance."

His presence filled the doorway. But this time instead of feeling threatened as she had the day she'd first seen him in the bed-and-breakfast, her pulse raced and happiness filled her from head to toe. He'd come back. She'd hoped and prayed he would and here he was.

She opened the door wide and gestured him inside.

"Merry Christmas, Amanda," he said as he walked past her into the living room.

She followed him into the room and stopped when he turned to face her. Firelight gleamed behind him, and she had flashes of another fire in another place that had resulted in a kiss that had changed her life.

He removed his cowboy hat, raked his hand through his hair and plopped the hat back on his head.

Amanda almost laughed out loud. She knew he only did that when he was nervous or tense or exasperated. She couldn't believe how wonderful it felt to see that doggone weathered old cowboy hat...or how much she had missed this particular cowboy. He was back—standing in her living room, shuffling his feet and looking like he wanted to be out in the great outdoors, somewhere, anywhere, instead of cooped up in her small living room which seemed to swallow up her gentle giant.

But she'd learned her lesson. No way was she going to let him walk out the door this time...not until she told him what was on her mind and in her heart.

"How have you been, Chance?"

He grinned that lopsided grin she so loved. "Shouldn't I be asking you that same question?"

She smiled back at him. "I'm fine." Her smile deepened. "Now." She gestured to the sofa. "Have a seat. Can I get you something to drink? It's cold outside. How about a mug of hot chocolate or a cup of warm apple cider?"

"No. Nothing. Thank you." He took off his hat and shuffled his feet.

Amanda had never seen this side of him before. He seemed almost shy, and she found it endearing.

Well, if he wouldn't sit and he didn't want anything to drink, then she was going to get straight to the point.

"Why are you here?" she asked. She gave him her most

loving smile and walked across the room stopping only an arm's length away.

He reached into his pocket, pulled out a small package and placed the gift in her hand. "Merry Christmas, Amanda."

She stared down at the festively wrapped present lying in her hand and then glanced up at him.

"Open it." He grinned.

"But I don't have a gift for you," she said.

"Ahh yes, you do." He closed the gap between them, pulled her into his arms and kissed her deeply, passionately.

She wrapped her arms around him, feeling the breadth of his shoulders beneath her hands.

Her cheeks flamed with heat, and her breath came in short little bursts of air when he finally released her.

"Go on," he said, gesturing to the box in her hand. His eyes were smoky, his voice husky. "Open it."

Not needing any further encouragement to rip away the wrapping paper, she stared at the small blue velvet jewelry box resting in her hand. Her stomach tied in knots. This wasn't…this couldn't be… She stared at the box and wasn't sure how to react. A wave of panic came over her. She knew without doubt that she was falling in love with this man…but they'd known each other for such a short time, and she didn't think she was ready…not yet…to say goodbye to her past and move on to her future. She didn't want to hurt Chance, but she didn't know if she could accept this gift…not yet, not now.

She raised her eyes to his.

"Trust me," he whispered, closing her hand around the box. "Just open it."

And then she saw it in his eyes…the empathy, the understanding, the caring.

Smiling up into his face, she brushed her lips lightly against his and then turned her attention to the small velvet treasure. She lifted the lid and gasped with delight when she saw the beautiful, delicate gold heart resting inside.

"It's beautiful, Chance. I love it."

He took the box from her and gently lifted the heart from inside it. "I wanted you to know that no matter what, you will always have my heart."

He lifted it higher, the firelight reflecting off the gold, and Amanda saw something etched on the back.

She reached out her hand and turned it over for a closer look.

"I had it engraved," Chance said, "with Alaska's state flower, the forget-me-not."

His expression sobered, and his eyes locked with hers. "I know we haven't known one another very long, Amanda." He laughed. "And I have to admit we met under less than perfect circumstances. But I'm hoping that…in time…maybe you'll come to have feelings for me."

Amanda lifted her hair off her neck and Chance stepped behind her and clasped the necklace in place. Both of them stared at the gold heart gleaming against her red turtleneck sweater.

"It's beautiful, Chance. Thank you."

"I know you have a lot of things to sort out, Amanda. I know you need time to really get to know me and decide what, if anything special, you might feel for me." His arms wrapped around her waist and his words whispered in her ear. "But I want you to know that I already know how I feel. Without question. Without doubt. I love you."

He turned her to face him without letting her out of his embrace. "And I'll wait, Amanda. As long as it takes. Because you are worth waiting for."

He caressed her cheek and then cupped the side of her

face with his hand. "Meanwhile, I just wanted you to know that you have my heart."

Amanda wrapped her arms around his waist, drawing herself closer and nuzzled the light beard growth on his face. "I love you, too."

She kissed him, this time with all the passion she possessed. When she came up for air, she grinned at him.

"I told you, Chance Walker. Christmas is God's promise of new beginnings."

Then she kissed him again.

EPILOGUE

Six months later

The summer sun shone bright, and Amanda adjusted her sunglasses against the glare as she walked through the cemetery. She found the grave without effort since she'd visited it several times over the past six months.

This time, however, would be her last visit. But her heart wasn't heavy. Somehow she knew that Edward would understand and be happy for her.

She glanced over her shoulder. Chance waited by the car at the bottom of the hill. Then she squatted down beside the grave.

"He's a good man, Edward. He's been good to me... and good for me." She sat down on the grass and traced her fingers across Edward's name on the headstone. "He's not a bounty hunter anymore. He opened his own security firm at the beginning of the year, and it is doing very well. And you'll never guess where." Amanda laughed out loud. "Yep. Fairbanks, Alaska.

"He bought a piece of property not far from the friends we made last winter. He had a house built. I can hardly wait to see it."

She glanced once more over her shoulder and then returned her attention to the grave.

"This will be the last time I'll be coming for a visit, Edward. But please know that I will always keep a special place in my heart just for you.

"I'm flying out a little later today with Chance. Our friends are standing up for us, and Annie has promised not to go into labor today. She absolutely promised me. You see, Chance and I are getting married today."

She smiled. "But somehow I think you already know that, don't you? And I know you're happy for me, Edward. I can feel it. That's just the kind of man you were. Kind. Compassionate. Loving."

Amanda stood up and brushed fresh-cut grass off her slacks.

"Thank you, Edward, for the brief time we had together."

She blew a kiss, placed a bouquet of fresh forget-me-nots against the smooth headstone and then turned and walked with joy and anticipation into her future.

* * * * *

Dear Reader,

Thank you so much for choosing *Bounty Hunter Guardian*. I hope you enjoyed the trials of Amanda and Chance as they fought for survival in the wilderness and escaped danger during their path to finding true love.

Personally, I've always been touched, at this time of year in particular, by Mary and Joseph's awesome faith in God's purpose and their total obedience to His plan.

As Amanda struggled through this Christmas season against her own almost insurmountable obstacles, I wanted to show how her unwavering faith and trust in the Lord not only brought her through the fire but how her example led Chance to find the Lord. I hope many people who come in contact with us in their daily lives see the presence of the Lord and open their hearts to His call.

I love hearing from readers. In January, 2012, I plan to start a quarterly newsletter to keep my readers up-to-date on what's going on in my world as I brainstorm new story ideas, finish my works-in-progress and promote books with free giveaway contests. If you'd like to subscribe, please send your email address to diane@dianeburkeauthor.com. I promise it will not be shared or used for any other purpose.

You can also find me on Facebook, on www.twitter.com/burkediane, and you can follow my blog, www.dianeburke.blogspot.com.

Blessings and a happy holiday to you and yours!

Diane Burke

QUESTIONS FOR DISCUSSION

1. Have you ever been unjustly accused of something you didn't do? How did it make you feel?

2. What is Chance's initial opinion of Amanda? How does that opinion change as he gets to know her?

3. Amanda is afraid to face the possibility that her husband may have been having an affair. How does this affect her decisions?

4. How does Amanda's deep faith impact Chance?

5. Amanda feels very alone but never gives up her belief that God has a plan for her life. Have you ever felt all alone? How did you cope with the feeling?

6. Many people who have not yet found their way to the Lord believe the Bible is merely an ancient book with no relevance in today's world. But Amanda finds her strength and inner peace by reading God's word. How does studying the Bible impact your life?

7. Chance has never known God in his life. How does Amanda help him come to the Lord? What makes Chance make the final decision to repent and welcome God into his heart?

8. Chance has lost his ability to trust people, including himself. How does this impact his actions and reactions in this story?

9. How does the story handle the themes of trust and forgiveness?

10. Discuss the motivations and actions of Mr. and Mrs. Stowe in the book and how their lives might have turned out differently if their hearts had been given to the Lord.

INSPIRATIONAL

Wholesome romances that touch the heart and soul.

SUSPENSE

COMING NEXT MONTH
AVAILABLE DECEMBER 6, 2011

DUTY TO PROTECT
Big Sky Secrets
Roxanne Rustand

SEASON OF DANGER
Hannah Alexander and Jill Elizabeth Nelson

HOLIDAY HIDEOUT
Rose Mountain Refuge
Lynette Eason

THE CHRISTMAS WITNESS
Susan Sleeman

REQUEST YOUR FREE BOOKS!

2 FREE RIVETING INSPIRATIONAL NOVELS
PLUS 2 FREE MYSTERY GIFTS

Love Inspired.
SUSPENSE

YES! Please send me 2 FREE Love Inspired® Suspense novels and my 2 FREE mystery gifts (gifts are worth about $10). After receiving them, if I don't wish to receive any more books, I can return the shipping statement marked "cancel". If I don't cancel, I will receive 4 brand-new novels every month and be billed just $4.49 per book in the U.S. or $4.99 per book in Canada. That's a saving of at least 22% off the cover price. It's quite a bargain! Shipping and handling is just 50¢ per book in the U.S. and 75¢ per book in Canada.* I understand that accepting the 2 free books and gifts places me under no obligation to buy anything. I can always return a shipment and cancel at any time. Even if I never buy another book, the two free books and gifts are mine to keep forever.

123/323 IDN FEHR

Name	(PLEASE PRINT)	
Address		Apt. #
City	State/Prov.	Zip/Postal Code

Signature (if under 18, a parent or guardian must sign)

Mail to the **Reader Service:**
IN U.S.A.: P.O. Box 1867, Buffalo, NY 14240-1867
IN CANADA: P.O. Box 609, Fort Erie, Ontario L2A 5X3

Not valid for current subscribers to Love Inspired Suspense books.

**Are you a subscriber to Love Inspired Suspense
and want to receive the larger-print edition?
Call 1-800-873-8635 or visit www.ReaderService.com.**

* Terms and prices subject to change without notice. Prices do not include applicable taxes. Sales tax applicable in N.Y. Canadian residents will be charged applicable taxes. Offer not valid in Quebec. This offer is limited to one order per household. All orders subject to credit approval. Credit or debit balances in a customer's account(s) may be offset by any other outstanding balance owed by or to the customer. Please allow 4 to 6 weeks for delivery. Offer available while quantities last.

Your Privacy—The Reader Service is committed to protecting your privacy. Our Privacy Policy is available online at www.ReaderService.com or upon request from the Reader Service.

We make a portion of our mailing list available to reputable third parties that offer products we believe may interest you. If you prefer that we not exchange your name with third parties, or if you wish to clarify or modify your communication preferences, please visit us at www.ReaderService.com/consumerschoice or write to us at Reader Service Preference Service, P.O. Box 9062, Buffalo, NY 14269. Include your complete name and address.

LISUS11B

When former Amishman Gideon Troyer sees his Amish ex-girlfriend on television at a quilt auction to raise money for surgery to correct her blindness, he's stunned and feels a pull drawing him back to his past.

Read on for a sneak preview of
THE CHRISTMAS QUILT
by Patricia Davids.

Rebecca Beachy pulled the collar of her coat closed against a cold gust of wind and ugly memories. An early storm was on its way, but God had seen fit to hold it off until the quilt auction was over. For that, she was thankful.

When she and her aunt finally reached their seats, Rebecca unbuttoned her coat and removed her heavy bonnet. Many of the people around her greeted her in her native Pennsylvania Dutch. Leaning closer to her aunt, she asked, "Is my *kapp* on straight? Do I look okay?"

"And why wouldn't you look okay?" Vera asked.

"Because I may have egg yolk from breakfast on my dress, or my back may be covered with dust from the buggy seat. I don't know. Just tell me I look presentable." She knew everyone would be staring at her when her quilt was brought up for auction. She didn't like being the center of attention.

"You look lovely." The harsh whisper startled her.

She turned her face toward the sound coming from behind her and caught the scent of a man's spicy aftershave. The voice must belong to an *Englisch* fellow. *"Danki."*

"You're most welcome." He coughed, and she realized he was sick.

"You sound as if you should be abed with that cold."

"So I've been told," he admitted.

"It is a foolish fellow who doesn't follow *goot* advice.

"Some people definitely consider me foolish." His raspy voice held a hint of amusement.

He was poking fun at himself. She liked that. There was something familiar about him, but she couldn't put her finger on what it was. "Have we met?"

*To see if Rebecca and Gideon can let go of the past
and move forward to a future together, pick up
THE CHRISTMAS QUILT by Patricia Davids
Available in December
from Love Inspired Books.*

Copyright © 2011 by Patricia MacDonald

SHLIEXP1211

As a teen, Lucas Clayton vowed never to return to Clayton, Colorado. Now he's back—with a child in tow—and no one is more surprised than Erin Fields, the sweetheart he left behind. But before he can convince Erin he's changed, he has to prove it to a young boy who needs a very special Christmas.

The Prodigal's Christmas Reunion
by Kathryn Springer

ROCKY MOUNTAIN HEIRS

Available December wherever books are sold.

www.LoveInspiredBooks.com

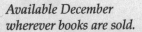